Thank you for purchasing, "The First 48 3: The Finale," Feel free to browse Amazon for the rest of my catalog, I hope you enjoy and thank you for the support. Below is a list of my previous work and social media contact.

- Forever my Savage: A Yungin and His Lady 1-4

- Daughter of a Trap King 1-4

- You Had No Mercy For My Soul 1 and 2 Finale

- She was a Savage, He was the realist 1-3

•Love Spells For The Goon I Adore

- Top Shottas

- Witches From The Eastside

- No Matter What, I Choose You 1 and 2 Finale

- Married to a New York Menace 1 and 2 Finale

- One Kiss For All My Troubles (A Standalone Novel)

•The Good Girl Who Loved A Savage 1 and 2 Finale

- I Got Love For A Philly Thug (A standalone novel)

Social Media Information

Facebook: Author Nakiala Comeaux and Giselle Gates

Instagram: @giselle_gates_author

Snapchat: Authorki16

Facebook Like Page : Giselle Gates

The First 48: Money Making Meeka 3
The Finale

By: Giselle Gates

Chapter 1

"WAKE UP, MOTHERFUCKA!" Rocko shouted. Rocko and Meeka sat in the wooden chair across from Philly staring at him. It was 2:45 in the morning and the wind was blowing heavily. Rocko felt like she was on top of the world. After trying to kill Philly on several different occasions, he was finally captured.

He tried to raise his head, but he was too dizzy. His black eyes were dripping a clear liquid and getting swollen by the second. He still managed to open one of them.

His bottom lip was split wide open. You could see the white meat showing. Rocko didn't care how bad he looked. Her eyes were glued to him, and he had all of her attention. It was kind of awkward to be in his presence and staring him in the eyes. She felt like she was finally facing her issues head-on.

"I swear I never saw this day coming. You gave me nightmares. When I thought about you, I would get sick for days. If I looked in the sand or ocean for too long, I would see your ugly little face. What you took from Kane I, I will hate you for forever. All of this started because of you! You always gave me bad vibes. I wish we would have never gotten into that car with you. One wrong move damaged our lives forever!!"

Rocko stared at Philly with a disgusted look on her face. His head was spinning, but he still managed to laugh. It made Rocko furious, and her blood started to boil. She jumped to her feet and slammed the muzzle of the gun into his chin. Blood splattered everywhere, and a piece of his chin fell to the floor. Seeing a piece of human flesh on the floor made Rocko's stomach weak. Rocko held her stomach and tossed her finger in the air. She hadn't seen a dead body in years or this much of blood.

"I'll be right back, Meek." She said and rushed out of the house. Meeka followed Rocko with her eyes and said, "Unlike her, seeing your shit busted open doesn't bother me. I've seen way worse than this. Anywho, you and I, we're going to have a nice little chit-chat.

"Oh, we are?" Philly asked.

"Yea, we are Philly," Meeka said.

"I ain't saying shit," Philly spit out a large amount of warm blood and laughed.

Meeka glanced at the blood on the floor and laughed with Philly. Meeka sat closer to him with her legs wide open. The smell of blood lingered heavily in the air. Meeka thought the odor would stay on her clothes.

"You're going to talk, trust me, Philly," Meeka said.

"If not, what the fuck are you going to do with me, kill me? I've seen everything besides death already. I'm not scared."

"You and me both, do you want a cookie? I am going to kill you though. Since I'm a good person, I'm going to let you choose how you want to die." Meeka laughed. "You can die a slow and painful death if you don't tell me what happened. Or you take one shot to the head if you tell me the truth. My aim is perfect, so I know exactly where to shoot you."

"Why should I tell you what happened? It doesn't make a difference. I'm going die anyway. So, I'm taking what happened to my grave."

"That's true, but let me tell you something else. You have caused sooooo much pain and heartache. You don't know the half of it. So many people want your head, it's ridiculous. We both can agree that you will not be missed. Your mom in California left you behind, and the rest of your family doesn't even know you exist. Your dad is on some island now on vacation with his new family. He doesn't give a fuck about you either. No one in your family cares about you because of all the pain you have caused. We can also agree that you are better off dead than alive." Philly's wide smile slowly faded away and became a frown. Meeka was ready to gloat, but she didn't. She knew talking about his family would break him down.

Rocko walked back into the house and stood by the door. Meeka signaled for Rocko to stay at the door. She shook her head and placed her hands on her hips.

Philly raised his head and spoke softly, "I didn't want to kill him, but I know you don't believe me. I'm not sure if it was the drugs or if I liked him. I can't lie and say I was hurt that I killed him. I've have known Kane's family for years, but I didn't think twice about killing his sisters and grandparents. Since you want to know the truth about Santana, I'll tell you…

Santana arrived in Scottsdale, Arizona with a huge smile on his face. It had been a month since he had seen Philly and he was missing him like crazy. It took him two hours to get dressed because he wanted to look perfect for Philly. His crimson red wig was parted down the middle and was styled bone straight. His nighttime makeup made his face seem slim, and his all-black dress exposed his figure.

Santana sped walked down the hotel halls searching for Philly's room. When he realized he was standing in front of room 202, he became more excited. He knocked on the door twice and waited for Philly to answer.

"Who is it?" Philly asked.

"It's Santana, open the door."

A few seconds later the door swung open. Santana stood there with his arms out and a huge smile on his face. Philly nodded his head and sat on the bed. He didn't seem too happy to see Santana.

"What's wrong with you?" Santana asked. He walked into the room and closed the door. Santana was flaunting his new hair around, but Philly ignored him.

"Nothing, I'm just tired." Philly rubbed his ashy face and laid across the bed. The hotel room was full of empty pizza boxes, dirty clothes, and crushed beer cans. The hotel room was so dirty Santana didn't want to sit on the bed.

"Are you sure? You seem a little....off." Santana said. Philly barely made eye contact with Santana when he spoke. He didn't want to admit it, but Santana could sense that something was wrong. It seemed like he was high and in a daze.

"I said I'm good. How was your flight?" Philly asked.

"Besides the woman sneezing the entire time and the crying baby, it was okay." He giggled.

"Oh, okay. Let's go and get something to eat. I'm starving, and I'm pretty sure you are too."

"Yea that's cool. Do you want me to drive? You seem tired." Santana asked.

"I'm not tired, and I'm not on any drugs today. I'm sober."

"Baby, how is your auntie?" Santana asked.

"Baby? Call me by my name. She's doing well. Thanks for asking." Santana walked side by side with Philly quietly. He tried to hold his hand, but Philly mean mugged him and pulled away.

"What are you doing?" Philly asked.

"Nothing, I was trying to hold your hand."

"Why?" Philly asked.

"Because I always hold your hand. What the hell is your problem today?"

"Nothing is my problem. Just stop with all of this gay shit!" Philly shouted. His loud outburst startled Santana and the front desk worker. He was a little embarrassed, so he gave her a fake wave. She smiled back and walked away from the front desk.

This was Santana's first time seeing Philly act in this manner toward him and he was a little hurt. He was usually a nice, caring, and affectionate person.

Philly pointed to a red 2008 Jeep Cherokee and said, "That's our ride right there."

"Okay," Santana said.

Santana and Philly got into the Jeep and drove through the empty hotel parking lot. Philly pointed left, so Santana turned left and drove down the road. It was dark and a little creepy. The awkward silence between them was bothering him, so Santana began to talk.

"I've been keeping my ears close to the streets like you said. No one is linking you to the robbery. Miami heard they picked up some guy from Eunice for questioning."

"Oh, that's what's up. I wasn't worried anyway."

"Good, that means you can come back home. I've been missing you like crazy." Santana smiled.

"I'll think about it, but I highly doubt it." Philly yawned loudly and covered his mouth while pointing to the left.

Santana made a left turn and asked, "What's to think about?"

"Maybe I don't want to go back home, ain't shit there but thots, trouble, and potholes."

"You should know. You're the one fucking the thots and causing the trouble." Santana laughed, and it made Philly angry. Philly raised his right hand and slapped Santana across the face.

BAM!

Santana slammed his foot on the brake and held his warm cheek. After he caught his breath, he pulled off. He was shocked that Philly hit him. He was puzzled and wasn't sure how to handle Philly's attitude.

"Don't ever say some stupid shit like that again! If you do, it's going to be way worse than a slap across the face."

"Ba-ba- baby I'm sorry. I was only joking with you, and you know that."

"What the hell did I tell you about calling me that dumb shit!" Philly slammed his hand against the dashboard and shouted. His loud shouting made Santana serve to the shoulder of the road. He quickly regained control of the wheel and made his way back to the road. Philly pulled his gun out and buried the muzzle into Santana's stomach.

Santana gasped and asked, "Philly, what are you doing?"

"What does it look like I'm doing? It's time for you to go!"

"Go where? Philly please..."

"Philly please what?" He laughed.

"Philly, please don't kill me. I'm literally begging you. I- I- I'll get in the middle of the road and beg you if you want."

"Get out of the car, NOW!"

Without replying, Santana threw the car into park and got out of the car. His legs felt numb, and he could feel butterflies in his stomach. For a moment, he thought about running, but he changed his mind. He knew Philly would gun him down and leave him in the middle of the road like road kill.

"WALK!" Philly shouted and hit Santana in the head with the gun. He staggered to the ground, but he managed to regain his balance. As he walked in the middle of the road, Philly shot Santana in the back.

"UUUUGGGHHHHHHHHH!" Santana moaned.

Santana begged for his life, but Philly didn't care. He continued to send shots into Santana's body. Once again, Philly took another body, and he wasn't bothered by it. Santana's body hit the ground with a thud and Philly ran the other way. He jumped back into the Jeep and drove off.

He drove the Jeep over Santana's body and laughed while shaking his head, "That nigga is still wearing that purse."

"No, no, no!" Rocko's hand and lips trembled as she listened to Philly tell them how he killed Santana.

Meeka and Rocko gasped. Hearing how Santana was killed made Meeka light headed. She wanted to break down and cry, but she had a job to do.

"I killed him because I was hired to. Not because he was gay. I don't know who made up that dumb rumor. He told me if I did it he would clear my criminal record of everything. It didn't matter what I did in the streets, he would get me out of it." Philly said.

"Who is he?" Rocko asked.

"Maybe I'm gay, shit, I don't know. It doesn't matter to me. As we all can see, I don't have anything to lose or to gain." Philly chuckled.

"WHAT! WHO PAID YOU TO KILL HIM?" Meeka shouted through a tight mouth. Philly laughed and spit blood out of his mouth. His mouth was running like a faucet. She poked his face with the gun and waited for him to give her an answer.

"Who do you think Tameeka? You're on the top of HIS hit list."

"AUSTIN?" Meeka asked. She could feel her heart starting to race, and she was becoming nervous.

"He's been plotting against you for a while now. He's been jealous of the relationship between you and Sydney. He knew by killing someone close to you it would break you. That's why he chose Santana." Philly replied.

POW! POW!

Meeka let two bullets go, and they entered his chest. His body along with the chair he was tied to fell backward, and he hit the dusty floor. Rocko was ready to throw up, but she held herself together. She ran to Meeka's side and asked, "Is he dead?"

"If this nigga took two bullets to the chest and isn't dead, I'm killing myself." Meeka raised her gun to Philly's head and let four shots go. Pieces of his head flew off.

Rocko didn't care that pieces of Philly's head was blown off. She continued to shoot until his head was completely blown off. She cried and sobbed because she felt like she was finally free. Apart of her past that she hated so much has finally vanished.

"Okay Rock, that's enough. Let's get the hell out of here!" Meeka snatched the gun out of Rocko's hand and pulled her by the arm. They ran out of the house, and neither of them looked back. Philly was finally dead.

They ran outside and got into the car, it was still running so they sped off. Meeka tried her best to control how her hands were shaking, but she couldn't. She swerved from left to right trying to get out of the high grass. Her heart was pounding so loud, she thought Rocko could hear it.

"Rocko, call Brink and tell him what's up," Meeka said.

"Okay." Rocko quickly dialed Hustle's number and waited for him to answer. On the first ring, he answered and said, "What's up?"

"The plan went through, and we're leaving now," Rocko said.

"Okay, we're on our way." Hustle said and disconnected the call. Rocko closed her eyes and laid her head against the window.

"Meeka, I feel free now. HE'S DEAD! PHILLY IS FINALLY DEAD!" Rocko shouted and clapped her hands.

"Yea, he's finally dead. Rest in peace Philly, you won't be missed." Meeka smirked and raised her eyebrows. Rocko closed her eyes and turned towards the window leaving Meeka in her thoughts. Half of her was happy that Philly was dead, but the other part of her wasn't bothered by his death. Killing Philly didn't bring Santana back nor would it change anything from her past. For a second, she regretted doing it.

"Do you think this was a mistake?" Meeka looked over toward Rocko as she drove, as Rocko's eyes grew big. She sat straight in her seat then she turned too left to face Meeka. While at the red light, Meeka couldn't face Rocko. She knew her question was stupid and it shouldn't have exited her mouth.

"Meeka are you serious?" Rocko laughed. Meeka laughed awkwardly and drove off. Rocko exhaled and shook her head.

"I'm joking girl. I'm glad we cleared that business. Now I have one more to go, and my hands will be clean. It's time to shut up all these bitch niggas."

"Who are you talking about and what do you have in mind?" Rocko asked.

"It's time I smoke Austin and get this shit over with. I can't have the devil riding my shoulders for much longer."

"Oh, word. You know I'm down for some grimy shit. What do you have in mind?"

"I don't have a full plan yet Rocko, but believe me when I say it will be grimy. Killing Austin is way past personal." Meeka said.

"How do you think Sydney is going to feel once she finds out he's dead?"

"I don't think she's going to care. She probably wants him dead as well. If she does say something, I'll put a bullet in her head as well." Meeka laughed loudly, but Rocko frowned. Meeka rolled her eyes and said, "Laugh a little Rocko, it was only a joke."

"A joke my ass. If you had to, I know you would smoke her."

"Well at least you know I'm telling the truth. I would hate to have another Justice situation. Her betrayal will always sit in the center of my heart like a dripping ice cube." Meeka said.

"Damn girl, that's deep on so many levels. Justice went out like Willie Lump-Lump, I can't even lie." Rocko laughed.

"Hell yea she did. I bet Willie is turning in his grave because of her." Meeka laughed and joked, but deep down, it wasn't funny to her. In the past week, Justice's death was on her mind all day.

"On another note Meeka, what's the plan now?" Rocko asked.

Meeka pulled into a hotel parking lot and put the car in park. Then she pulled the keys out the ignition and leaned back against her seat. Rocko didn't say much, but Meeka knew what she was referring too.

"The plan is to kill Austin and continue to get this money. What else is new in society?" Meeka replied and laughed.

"It doesn't sound like the plan Hustle has in mind."

"I know, but it's the best plan I can think of. I'm hot right now, and I can't stop with this escorting shit. Backpage is booming. I have bitches taking over hotel rooms and boulevards in twelve states. I would be a fool to let it go that easily." Meeka said.

"Okay girl. It's your life, and you know better than me. Just know this, when Hustle leaves your ass, you can move in with us." Rocko laughed.

"Move where, to Bora Bora?" Meeka asked.

"Well duh, I damn sure don't live in Opelousas anymore."

"Uuhhhh, I think I'll past. The last thing on my mind is being worried about that. Hustle loves me too much to leave me. I know this in my heart. I have no worries." Meeka said.

"Just because YOUR mouth says that that doesn't mean his heart says the same. Women get tired of waiting around, and so do men. Don't be a fool and think you can have your cake and eat it too."

Meeka wanted to reply, but her phone began to ring. She thought it was Hustle, but instead, it was Sydney. Meeka pressed the screen and said, "Hello?"

"Meeka can you talk? Shit went down at the club!" Meeka's heart dropped to the floor, and she held her chest. By the tone of Sydney's voice and the way she was breathing heavily, Meeka knew something bad had happened.

"WHAT THE FUCK HAPPENED SYDNEY? TALK TO ME NOW, I NEED FULL DETAILS AND DON'T LEAVE ANYTHING OUT."

"The club got raided!"

"Oh my God, are you serious? How did this happen?" Meeka asked.

"I'm very much serious Meeka, and you can thank Vixen's money hungry ass for this. I told her that new guy looked suspicious and to stick to the tricks she knew. But noooo, she didn't want to listen to me. Vixen said the man had $4,000 and wanted to take her to the Champagne Room. I watched the entire thing happen. As soon as he handed her the money, the cuffs were coming right behind it. About four other undercover cops came out of nowhere. When I spotted the cuffs, I ran out the back door. Right now I'm driving home in seven inch clear heels and a two-piece bikini. It is freezing tonight, but I'm glad I made it out of there!"

"I'm glad you were on the lookout. If you were booked, Austin would have eaten that shit up." Meeka said.

"You got that right Meeka. I was surprised he wasn't in there. In the back of my mind, I think he was the one who set it up. The last time the club was raided was in 2009. My nigga, we're in what year now, something just isn't adding up." Sydney shook her head and placed her car in park at the stop sign. Then she reached under her seat for her .38 handgun and dropped it on the passenger's side seat. She then turned around and shuffled through the pile of clothes that covered the back seat. She found one of Xavier's hoodies and quickly pulled it over her head. The smell of his cologne made her miss him a little. Things were still a little rocky between them, mostly on her side. She loved Xavier so much, and the pain of him cheating on her was hurtful. Sydney wasn't sure which direction things were going to go between them. Her heart still held a great amount of love for him. On the contrary, being a 'single' woman was fun, and Jason made her feel young again.

"Hello, Sydney is you still there?" Meeka asked.

"Yea Meeka, I'm still here. I was putting a hoodie on. I had to cover my boobies. It was no way in the world the headlines would have said my name. I can see it now, 'Saint Landry Parish teacher apart of strip club raid.' Hell to the no times two. I wasn't having that." Sydney laughed.

"This shit is crazy man. I need to call Matthew as well. I know he isn't there now because he is at home sick. Are you home yet?"

"No, but I'll be at YOUR house in about ten minutes." Sydney tried moving back home, but it didn't work. Every time she stepped foot in her bedroom, she saw Xavier making love to another woman. It didn't matter how many times he said he was sorry, the damage was still done. Until she could get a place of her own, she was living at Meeka's other house. Sydney felt like a charity case, but Meeka didn't see it that way. Sydney was her best friend, and she wanted to help her in any way that she could. "Okay Meek, I'll call you back."

"Okay, talk to you later." Meeka disconnected the phone call and dropped her head on the steering wheel. Too many thoughts were racing through her head, and she couldn't gather any of them. "What the fuck!" Meeka whispered under her breath and shook her head. She needed to call Hustle and let him know what happened. Meeka could only imagine the things Hustle would say.

"That's a warning sign Meeka, don't be stupid," Rocko said.

"Shut up Rocko and go back to Bora Bora." Meeka joked.

***

Now that Meeka was back at home, she needed to pay a visit to Justice's mom, Mary. She tried her best to avoid her, but Mary called Meeka's phone nonstop while she was away. She considered Meeka her daughter and wanted her to be the shoulder she cried on. Meeka was tired of the fake tears, but she didn't mind pushing out a few more to play the part.

Meeka took a bite of the banana pudding she was eating and washed it down with a cold glass of milk. Mary sat next to Meeka clutching a rosary and a picture of Justice close to her heart. Meeka took another bite of the banana pudding then she sat the plate on the coffee table. She wiped the corners of her mouth and said, "Mrs. Mary, your banana pudding is delicious."

"Thank you Tameeka. I know it's your favorite so I decided to make it." She cracked a smile.

"I appreciate that. You know I only eat your banana pudding." She laughed.

"You sound exactly like Justice when you said that. I miss my baby so much Tameeka. This is hard to cope with. I don't understand what kind of secret life she was living, but Justice didn't deserve to be killed."

"No one, especially Juju deserved to be killed. Whoever did this left her for dead? Only a heartless person would do something like that." Meeka said.

"You're right about that Tameeka, a cruel and heartless person."

"Did yall get any more leads about anything?" She asked.

"No nothing new since the last time. I know they are saying that Miami girl did it, but I don't believe it." Mary said.

"Why not?" Meeka asked.

"I don't believe it because that was her friend. I can't see a friend doing something vicious like that."

"I can see it, Mrs. Mary. Friends aren't always friends." Meeka said.

"Do you believe that she did it Tameeka?" Mary asked.

"Yes I do, but at the end of the day, I can't prove it. Miami is dead also, and we'll never get a confession. With a confession or not, just know that I'm here for you. We're going to get through this together." Meeka said as she sat closer to Mrs. Mary and rubbed her hands. Meeka's soft eyes and beautiful face comforted Mary to the highest extent.

"She always talked about how you were a good friend to her. You, Justice, and Santana were like the three amigos. How is his mom by the way?"

"She's doing the best she can do. I can only imagine how it feels to lose a child. I would lose my mind if I lost my sweet baby Isabella. Matter of fact, before I leave, I'll give you her number. You two could help one another out in this time."

"Oh that would be nice Tameeka, thank you so much. I know this has to be hard on you as well. In a year, you have lost both of your best friends. I don't know how you are still standing. I probably would have lost my mind by now."

"I deal with it the best way I can. I know that Santana and Justice wouldn't want me with my head hanging low. Sometimes when I'm alone, I cry, and I swear I can hear them. I know it sounds crazy, but it's healing my soul."

"I understand that that means they are in your presence. Don't be scared of it Tameeka, embrace it."

"You're right, and I will do that." Meeka smiled.

"How is your baby doing by the way? I haven't seen that little pretty girl in a while."

"She's doing well and growing every day. The next time I visit you, I'll make sure to bring her with me."

"Okay and what about that boyfriend of yours, how is he?" She asked.

"Brink is good. He actually has Isabella now. Have you spoken to Pedro lately? Brink and I called his phone a few times this week, but he hasn't answered." Meeka asked.

"Hmmm, I haven't spoken to Pedro in two weeks, now that I think of it. I tried calling him, but he didn't answer or return my phone call either."

"Wow, that's crazy, and that's not like him at all. I'm going to call Brink, and we're going to pass by his house."

"Please do that and let me know." She said.

"Ummm, is Austin coming to get some of this banana pudding? If not, I want to take the whole pan." Meeka joked. The last thing on her mind was taking the banana pudding home. This was her way to start a conversation about Austin. Meeka hadn't seen Austin since she has been home and she wanted a little information on him. Meeka couldn't say much about Austin. Mary was clueless about everything that was going on between him, her, Justice, and Sydney. In her mind, Sydney and Austin were going through a clean and smooth divorce.

"I don't think so. He took a few days off from work."

"Oh really, is he on vacation?" She asked.

"He went to Pensacola, Florida to visit some family," Mary said.

"Pensacola, I didn't know you guys had family there?"

"We don't, that's family on his dad's side. He said he would be back today." Mary said.

"Oh okay, well before it gets too late, I'm going to make a stop by Pedro's house."

"Let me know if he's there or not Tameeka, please."

"Yes ma'am and have a good day. I promise we will get through this together." Meeka took one more bit of her banana pudding and gave Mary a hug. She squeezed Meeka tightly around the waistline and gave her a kiss on the cheek. Her maroon lipstick left a big lip print on Meeka's cheek, but she didn't care.

"I want you to know something, I pray for you every night. I hope that nothing happens to you in these crazy streets."

"As long as you continue to pray for me, nothing will happen. Besides, I have Justice and Santana as my guardian angels."

"You are right about that Tameeka. Take care of yourself."

"I will," Meeka stood to her feet and walked to the door. Her heart dropped when she closed the front door and saw Austin standing there. When he noticed it was Meeka at the door, a mean mug took over his face. He rushed out of his car and charged her way. Meeka exhaled and walked to her car. She reached for the door handle, but Austin grabbed her by the bicep. Meeka glanced at her arm and then up at Austin, but he didn't release her arm. She started to laugh and wiggled her head.

"I heard you were on a little vacation. How was your trip Austin?" Meeka asked.

"That's none of your damn business."

"What's with the attitude Austin?" She asked sarcastically, but it made Austin furious. He grabbed her arm tighter and applied more pressure.

"I should have killed you months ago, but my sister was obsessed with you. She was basically in love with you as if you were some kind of saint. All you are is the devil in cheesy designer clothes. You should donate some of that drug money to charity instead showing off."

"I would tell you the same, but your checks are shitty. I donated $5,000 to the Boys and Girls Club, but what do you do, besides finding money hungry lil' niggas and turning them into rats? What are you honestly doing for the community?" Meeka laughed.

"Shut the fuck up, you stupid bitch. I swear on my life, I never liked you."

"The streets say different, they love me." Meeka licked her lips and seductively bit her bottom lip. Austin was right, he hated her, and she could basically smell it on his breath.

"Let's see how long it's going to be before the streets start to hate you too."

"Everyone loves me, including your family. Your mom made me a delicious pan of banana pudding. You should try some." She laughed.

"Bitch you have some nerve to still come around here!"

"Excuse me, if you know like I know, you would let go of my arm," Meeka snatched her arm from his hand and pushed him away.

"Why, are you going to shoot me how you did Juju?" The look of a crazy man was buried deep in Austin's eyes, but that didn't mean Meeka was going to fold under pressure.

"You should have asked Miami that, not me," Meeka said.

"Trust me I know you killed my sister. No one or any evidence can make me believe Miami did it."

"I don't know what you're talking about. The evidence clearly shows that Miami did it and why would I kill my own friend? I loved the girl like a sister. I loved her more than you did!!" Meeka knew to be careful with her choice of words. She wasn't sure if Austin had a wire attached to his body or not so she wasn't taking any chances.

"I'll get to the bottom of it. I don't care if I don't have evidence."

"Have a good day Detective Austin, and I'm sorry for your loss." Meeka got into her car and quickly backed out of the driveway. It was time to kill Austin and get it over with. In her heart, she knew Austin would do anything to pend Justice's death on him.

She reached for her phone to call Hustle, but he was calling her.

"Right on time," Meeka cleared her throat and answered the call. She had plenty to tell Hustle, but she wasn't sure where to start.

"Hello?"

"What's up baby, where are you?" Hustle asked.

"I'm leaving Mrs. Mary's house and bbbaabbbyyyyyy, do I have a lot to tell you!"

"Damn, did something bad happen and do I need to come there?" Hustle asked.

"Austin and I got into an argument while I was leaving Mrs. Mary's house. He said he knows," Meeka thought about it for a second and stopped talking. This wasn't something she should talk about on the phone. Meeka was tempted to throw the phone out of the window, but she didn't. This was the third phone she purchased this month and Hustle was jumping down her throat for each phone. "Ummm, where are you?"

"I'm home, but why did you stop talking?" He asked.

"I don't want to talk about that right now. What I do want to talk about is Pedro. Mrs. Mary said she hasn't spoken to him in two weeks. Baby, don't you find that strange that no one has spoken to him?" Meeka asked.

"Yes I do, and I need to figure it out. I wanted to give him time to grieve but time is up."

"I'm glad you said that because I told Mrs. Mary I was going to pass by his house. Can you meet me there?" She asked.

"Yea, I'll be there in a few minutes."

"Okay."

Five minutes later, Meeka arrived at Pedro's house. A few seconds later, Hustle was pulling in his driveway as well. Pedro's car was gone so he couldn't be home. Meeka pulled her phone out and dialed his number. His number was no longer in service and Meeka was shocked.

As Meeka got out of the car, she dialed Pedro's number again. The recording said that the number was disconnected, again. "Baby when is the last time you called his phone?" She asked.

"Yesterday I think, why?" He asked.

"Because I just called and it's saying the number is no longer in service," Meeka dialed Pedro's number and handed Hustle the phone. He held it against his ear and listened to the operator. Hustle removed the phone from his ear and stared at the screen.

"What the fuck! Are you sure this is his number?" Hustle asked.

"I'm pretty sure it is. It does say, Pedro."

"Well, something isn't right, and I'm going to find out today." Hustle grabbed Meeka by the arm and walked through Pedro's front yard. She tucked her phone in her back pocket and tiptoed through the high grass. Pedro was a neat freak, and it was unusual to see his lawn a mess. The weeds were growing out of control, and the uncut grass reached right above their ankles.

"There is no way Pedro has been home. Look at his yard, it's a mess. That boy cuts his lawn twice a week and sometimes three times a week."

"That's how I know something is wrong," Hustle said as he was about to knock on the door until he noticed that it was already slightly open.

"What the fuck!" Meeka took a step back, and Hustle reached on his hip for his gun. With his free hand, he grabbed the doorknob and pushed the door open.

"I don't like this at all Brink!" Meeka whispered.

"Ayo Dro, are you in here?" Hustle shouted from the door. The house was stuffy, and a stale smell filled the air. Pedro didn't reply so Hustle pulled his gun out and walked inside the house. Meeka followed behind him and opened the door wider. She couldn't tolerate much of the heavy odor.

Hustle looked around the living room, but nothing seemed out of place. He took a few steps closer to the kitchen and squinted his eyes. A few dirty dishes filled the sink, but nothing alerted him. Just because nothing concerned him, that didn't mean he was leaving right away. He continued to walk in the kitchen, and he opened the icebox. The smell of sour milk slapped him in the face, and he quickly closed the icebox door.

"What is it Brink?" She asked.

"Sour milk, that's all."

"It's hot as hell in this house. I sure hope he isn't living in this hot box," Meeka wiped the sweat from her and raised her arms in the air. She waved under each arm and sniffed her armpits. The house was so hot she was beginning to smell musty.

"Clearly Pedro isn't here. I think we should leave and come back later." Meeka implied, but Hustle ignored her.

"Something...doesn't feel right Meek. I'll check his bedroom to see what I find." Hustle said.

"I'll check the bathroom also. Maybe I'll find something in there," Meeka and Hustle walked in different directions and entered the rooms. Meeka opened the medicine cabinet and noticed that all of Pedro's toiletries were gone. She walked out of the room and shouted, "Hustle all of Pedro's toiletries are gone!" Meeka walked into the room and found Hustle sitting on the edge of the bed. A blank look was on his face, and a sheet on paper was in his hand.

"What's wrong baby?" Meeka asked.

"This letter answers some of our questions, but not much," Hustle exhaled and handed Meeka the letter. The letter was covered with Pedro's handwriting, she began to read it.

If you're reading this letter, then that means you've realized that I'm gone. Don't try and look for me. I'm good. Dealing with Justice's death is hard, and I don't know how to deal with it. I'm not sure if I'm ever coming back. I probably won't.

Peace.

Meeka read Pedro's letter twice and shook her head. She tried to read between the lies, but the letter was short, simple, and straight to the point. She sat next to Hustle and handed him the letter. They locked eyes with one another, but no one knew what to say. Meeka couldn't say anything, Pedro was gone, and that was the end of that.

***

Tonight was an emotional and hard day for everyone. On top of Pedro disappearing without a trace, Forty dropped a major bombshell on everyone. He decided to move to Florida with his auntie Maryland for good. Meeka felt like his decision was too soon, but she couldn't do anything but respect it.

"Today was a crazy day. I need more than a drink," Sydney rubbed her face and crossed her legs tightly. She couldn't believe that Pedro was gone. She had to see it for herself.

"I second that, but I'm not doing any dope." Meeka joked.

"Hell no, maybe a little weed and that's it." Sydney laughed.

"Maybe a Tab too so I can throw it back. Then I'll forget about all of this."

"Just like in the cartoons, I'm not sure who shocked me more, Dro or Forty. I understand why Forty chose to leave. It's a good move for him. He's young, but he's been through so much. I'm surprised he hasn't turned to drugs. I know I would have." Sydney said.

"Nah, not Forty, he's a strong kid. He has sold enough drugs to see and know what they can do to you." Meeka said.

"I still can't believe Forty left. I'm going to miss him. I still don't feel comfortable letting Austin around the boys. Even though Xavier and I are rocky right now, I still like that he is active in their lives. That's one of his good qualities; he didn't let us ruin his relationship with the boys." Sydney took a sip of her peach daiquiri and crossed her legs.

"I do give him that. Most men would have said fuck them, kids." Meeka said.

"When I was back in college I never imagined my life would be like this. I'm in the middle of a divorce, an undercover stripper, screwing someone that's half my age, and my relationship is going through some crazy things. On top of that, I have one foot in the grave and one in the jail."

Every word that exited Sydney's mouth cut her deep. Meeka felt like she was responsible for all the bad in Sydney's life. Before Meeka came along, Sydney was struggling just like Justice. She was fresh out of graduate school and a struggling 2nd-grade teacher. Meeka introduced her to the strip club, and from that day forward that was all she knew. Being a teacher is what she loved and had a passion for, but it didn't allow her to live the lifestyle she wanted.

Meeka and Sydney sat on her bed deciding what Sydney should wear to work tomorrow. She hated visiting Sydney and Austin's house, but she didn't want to hurt Sydney's feelings by telling her that. The one-bedroom house was a shack and needed major reconstruction done to it. Several holes filled the floor and Meeka often spotted cockroaches throughout the house. Every time Sydney cooked Meeka's favorite food; gumbo, she offered Meeka some, but she always found a way to turn it down. There was no way Meeka would eat a thing that came from that house. Just because Sydney was her friend didn't mean that the roaches and rats were her friends.

"I wish you would come with us to Miami," Meeka said.

"Me too, I need a vacation, but you know I can't afford that right now." Sydney pouted.

"I can loan the money to you Sydney. You know that."

"No thank you Meeka. I'll just save up for the next trip." Sydney said.

Sydney and her husband were struggling and could barely maintain their rent. Meeka offered to help on several occasions, but Austin always declined the offer. Sydney was so head over heels in love that she obeyed what her husband said.

"I guess Sydney," Meeka looked around the cluttered room and secretly shook her head. The sheets had permanent stains on them, and it disgusted Meeka. It made Meeka push to the edge of the bed and sit tight.

"I guess Tameeka." Sydney rolled her eyes and walked to her closet. She gently pulled the closet door back because it was barely hanging on the hinges.

"I don't know why it takes us an hour to figure out what you should wear. You only have like six pieces of clothes. Two blouses, three bottoms, and a damn dress. A dress that I hate with a passion because olive is not your color. I keep telling you that girl," Meeka grabbed the long dress and gagged. Then she pulled it off the hanger and

tossed it to the trash can. Sydney gasped and ran to the dress.

"Come on now Tameeka. That was rude and unnecessary."

"I'm sorry girl, but I strongly hate that dress," Meeka pulled the dress that she had on over her head and brushed her hand down it. She stood in the center of the room in her bra and biker shorts. It was a little cold in the room, but Meeka didn't care. The dress was not that important to her, but she knew it would mean a lot to Sydney. She couldn't remember the last time she saw Sydney purchase a new piece of clothing and she was long overdue for something new.

"No Meeka put your dress back on."

"It's not my dress anymore. I'm going shopping when I leave from here. If Hustle sees me with that dress on, he's going flip out anyway." Meeka laughed.

"Are you sure, this dress looks expensive?" Sydney held the red dress in mid-air and examined it. The material was thick but soft. This dress could last her all year and probably the next year.

"Girl no, I caught it on the clearance rack at Rainbow. It was $5.99, and I got one in blue as well." Meeka lied, the dress cost $200, but Sydney didn't need to know that.

"Oh okay, thanks Meeka. Good looking out. Next time they have a sell I hope I have some free money." She said.

"You wouldn't have to worry about that if you let me put you in a position to get money. I know you don't

want to take money from me and I get that. Do I understand, kind of, you want to be independent right?"

"It's not about being independent Meek. Taking money from you wouldn't be right. It makes my husband feel like less of a man, and that's drug money. How would a cop look spending drug money?"

"He doesn't have to know Sydney. I hate that you live in this rat hole. Teaching is cute, but it doesn't put you ahead. I want you to be ahead, you deserve that."

"Everything is going to work out, trust me. Once I pay my student loans off and recover my bank account from the wedding, we will be okay. We won't have money like you, but we'll have a decent roof over our head." She said.

"Sydney look, this shit is fucked up, and it's time for me to fix it. I have a side job for you, and it could put you on your feet in no time! If you hustle right, fifty percent of your student loans will be paid off." Meeka said.

"Thank you Tameeka, but I am not selling drugs. I will not risk my career over a few rocks."

"Naw, I don't sell drugs like that. That's Hustle's thing. I'm all about selling pussy, well, other women's pussy."

"You mean prostituting? I'm not selling my body!"

"Sydney, stop talking and let me explain. A few of my hoes are dancing at the club in Lafayette called He He's. That's just their way to fuck in clubs instead of going to a hotel room. It's smarter, safer, and an easier way to build their clientele. Miami went from driving a 1993 Honda to a 2003 Benz. I'm cool with the owner, and I can get you in the club with no problem. You only have to

dance two nights out of the week, and no one has to ever know."

"Just two nights?" She asked.

"Yep and I'll explain to him about your job," *Meeka said.*

"NO ONE will know?"

"No one will know unless you tell them. I've seen the girls do it all the time Syd. It's not that bad. Some just shake their ass and look pretty on stage. They don't even come out of their clothes. Half the time you can't recognize who is who because of the wigs and makeup they wear. Think about it hard, this could be your come up. You can do it for a few days or weeks. No one said you had to retire as a stripper."

"I don't know Meek. I don't know how to dance. I don't want to get on stage and look like a fool."

"You won't look like a fool, I got you. Now stand in front of the mirror, and I'll show you a few things."

"You know how to strip?" Sydney asked and laughed.

"Of course I do. How do you think I keep Hustle around," she joked.

"Hmmm, it must be nice. Everyone can't be like you; young and gettin' and you're dating Hustle! I know that nigga is breaking bread with his fine ass," Sydney rubbed her hands against her cheeks and licked her lips.

Meeka sized her up and down and said, "Bitch don't play, that's all me."

"That's all you for now. We all know you don't keep a man for long." Sydney laughed.

"I think I'm going to keep this one for a while. Besides being a handsome ass fella, Hustle is a good dude. I can see him and I having a bunch of pretty curly head babies." Meeka laughed.

"If you say so, but don't break that man's heart. You know you can be a bitch majority of the time."

"You're right about that, but we'll see how things go. I'll never know until I try something out. Let's hope he doesn't break my heart. You know women cling to him like flies at a barbeque."

"Let me guess, you're referring to what happened last week?" Sydney turned around with her hands on her hips. Meeka turned away and snickered.

Last week, Meeka got into a little altercation with one of Hustle's ex-girlfriends. She called Hustle's phone non-stop saying disrespectful things about Tameeka. Once Meeka finally ran into her, things got ugly and out of hand. Since the altercation, the girl hasn't called Hustle's phone again.

"Don't start your shit, Syd. Mike deserved to get her arm and nose broken. First of all, what kind of women is named Mike? For a minute, I thought it was a man texting his phone, and he was gay."

"Well, whatever the case is, you need to stay out of trouble Meeka. Your name is ringing in these streets heavily girl."

"As long as that money continues to roll in like it is, my name can just ring," Meeka pulled a stack of money out of her pocket and smiled. She wanted to hand the money to Sydney, but she knew she wouldn't take it. Sometimes Meeka would purposely lose money hoping Sydney would *find it. Sometimes she did and sometimes she didn't. Even when she didn't, Meeka hoped someone else did.*

"Is it worth it?" Sydney asked.

"Is what worth it?" Meeka asked.

"Having your name all in the streets and jeopardizing your freedom like that?"

"Yea it is worth it when I get to feed Justice, Marlo, and Santana. Yea, they're eating, but I need to get them in a position where they can eat without me." Meeka said.

"Seems like that Justice girl likes riding your coat tail."

"What?"

"You heard what I said. It looks like she's spending more money than saving."

"You're talking like you don't fuck with Juju. I thought you two were cool?" Meeka asked.

"She's a cool chick, and I don't have a problem with her. I'm just calling it how I see it. I rather you be your own downfall, instead of someone else's."

"I guess Syd, but get in front of the mirror so I can show you a few things. If you want me to, I can talk to the manager tonight, and he can squeeze you on the roster." Sydney didn't say anything. She was deep in her thoughts. She couldn't picture herself shaking her ass or even in a strip club, but she was desperate for the money. It felt like every day the bills were increasing, and she couldn't catch a break.

"Okay, that's cool. Austin can't know about this, okay?"

"If you won't tell him, I sure won't. Now get in front of the mirror and show me something." Meeka laughed.

Meeka stood behind Sydney, and she could hear her heart pounding. She was so uptight. Meeka knew touching on Sydney made her uncomfortable, but she had to get her prepared for the strip club. Meeka never danced on stage before, but she spent enough time in the strip club and knew enough about how to move.

"All you have to do is feel the beat and tap into your inner freak," Meeka pulled Sydney's long hair behind her shoulders and made her do a body roll. At first, she didn't have any rhythm, but after a while it became natural.

"Can I ask you something and be honest with me?"

"What is it?" Sydney asked.

"Do you blame me for your life being this way?" Meeka asked.

"What?" Sydney laughed.

"I'm serious Syd. Do you blame me for your life being this way? If so, I won't get upset. I'll take full responsibility for my actions." Meeka asked.

"Why would I blame you for my life being like this? I'm the reason it spiraled out of control, and I take full responsibility for it. I was a grown ass woman, and you were a child at the time. You couldn't make me do nothing I didn't want to do. I fell in love with the lifestyle, and I didn't want to stop it. I never want you to think that again, okay?" Sydney said.

"I don't know. I just feel like that."

"But I don't feel like that. I love you Meek, and you know that" Sydney stood to her feet and gave Meeka a hug.

"I love you too Syd, and I mean that. Right about now, Justice would have been here with us. This shit gets crazier by the second," Meeka said as she shook her head and rubbed her eyes. Thinking about Justice or even talking about her always put her in a weird place. Even though she didn't like talking about it, sometimes it was a must to get her feelings off her chest.

"Yep and talking shit. In this moment, she would be standing in the fridge doorway twerking and rapping." Sydney laughed.

"She would freestyle about the shit in the fridge. That girl was a clown and a half." Meeka clapped her hands and laughed.

"Is it wrong to say I miss her?" Sydney asked.

"No, because I miss her too. Why did she have to do this to us?"

"I'm going to bed, goodnight Meek." Sydney took one more sip of her drink and gave Meeka the peace sign. Meeka did the same and reached for the remote for the TV. As Sydney walked to the bedroom, Meeka increased the volume on her television. She watched the news for a few minutes then she stood to her feet. Her body felt warm, and she was ready to get in bed. Meeka quietly walked into her room and climbed into bed. Hustle was sleeping, and she didn't want to wake him up, so she decided to leave the television off.

It was 2:45 in the morning and Meeka's emotions were taking over her. It didn't matter how much she tried to sleep, the demons she was fighting didn't allow her to. She wasn't sure if it was the conversation with Austin, Mary, or

Pedro's reason for leaving, but Justice was on her mind heavily. That explained why she felt guilty and sick to her stomach. Her body was drenched in sweat, but she was also trembling. She prayed that the wet sheets and chattering of her teeth didn't wake Hustle. Meeka's guilty conscious was eating her alive, and for the first time, she was ready to crack.

As she laid on her stomach, tears filled her eyes. Meeka wanted to keep quiet, but she couldn't any longer. She grabbed Hustle's hand and placed it on her chest. The dampness of her sports bra and her pounding heart frighten Hustle. His eyes grew big, and he turned on his side to face Tameeka. Meeka started to hyperventilate. She tried her best to control her breathing. She turned to Hustle, and her tears fell onto her shoulders. Neither one of them knew what to do, but Meeka held his hand tightly.

"Baby, what's wrong?" He asked.

"I – I – I don't know baby. I think I need to…go to the hospital."

"Why, what's the problem? Are you in pain?" He asked.

"I'm not in pain." She whispered.

"So what's the problem? Talk to me, tell me something. I need to fix whatever the problem is."

Meeka grabbed the sides of her bra and pulled it over her head. She was disgusted at how the sweat dripped from the bra. Hustle grabbed it and dropped it on the floor. He wiped his wet hands on his silk pillowcase and mumbled, "What the fuck, why are you so sweaty?"

"I think it's my guilt messing with me. I've been thinking about Juju all night, and I haven't gotten any sleep."

"Why?"

"I don't know why Brink! If I had all the answers, you would know! What if I took her life for no reason? What if she was pretending to work just to fool Austin? What if she was on my side the entire time? I may have fucked up big time, and now I can't redo it! Her family took her death hard, and I had to pretend like I was hurt but in reality, I wasn't at all. How could I care when I'm the one who killed her? I've done messed up some things before, but this is the worse."

"I understand you feel like this sweetheart. You are human. This wasn't a random person you killed. She was your best friend. I don't expect you to move on from it and act like it didn't happen. On the other hand, what she did was cutthroat. I remember watching you take that bitc…"

"Don't call her a bitch Brink, that's disrespectful!" Meeka tossed her hands in mid-air and rolled her eyes. Hustle grabbed her one of her hands and gave it a wet kiss.

"I'm sorry. I was out of line for that. I remember watching you take that girl out of the slums, and that was how she repaid you?"

"Right," Meeka whispered.

"If I was in your shoes, I would have done something way worse. I probably would have tortured her and made her beg for her life."

"I know this is going to be a shocker, but I don't have the heart to do that." She laughed.

"That's why I always see the good in you. It doesn't matter what people say about you. There's some good in that black heart of yours," Hustle rubbed his hand against her chest and chuckled.

"That's the problem you are the only person that sees good in me. It doesn't matter what good I do, they only know me for the bad. I wish they would see me the way you see me. When Isabella gets older, I can only imagine what they will tell her about me. I know she's going to hate me."

"You are not a bad person baby so stop saying that. She's going to know you as the world's best mom and her best friend. I don't think there is anything someone can say about you that will make her hate you."

"Wow, it seems like you have all of the answers to everything. It must be nice."

Meeka raised her eyebrows and tucked her hair behind her ears. Hustle pulled Meeka close to his body and kissed her forehead. She wanted to show him affection, but the salty smell of sweat covered her body. Instead, she held his hand and kissed his cheek.

"I don't have all the answers, but I can state facts. Are you feeling better?" Hustle asked.

"Yea, I am, but I'm cold. The shower is calling my name." Without replying, Hustle stood to his feet and scooped Meeka up in his arms. As he walked to the bathroom, he pulled her white lace panties off and dropped them to the floor. Once he had made it to the bathroom, he flicked the light on and placed Meeka on the toilet. Her naked body shivered, and she was ready to feel the hot water against her body.

"Thank you, Brink." She whispered.

"What?" He asked.

Meeka rubbed the middle of her throat and said, "I said thank you."

"You're welcome. But thank me for what?" Hustle turned the hot and cold water on then he ran his hand under it. He wanted to make sure it wasn't too cold or hot.

"Everything you do for me. I love you so much."

"Aawww, I love you too baby. While you're in the shower, I'll get your clothes and check on Izzy."

"Cool," Meek stepped into the shower, and she didn't waste any time letting the water cover her. She walked in a circle and let the water wet her hair. The water felt great, just as she expected, but it didn't take her mind off Justice.

A vivid picture of Justice's dead body appeared in her head. She tried to shake the thought out. She tried to think about something else, but she couldn't. The image appeared over and over, but this time, she was starting to freak out. All of a sudden, she could hear Justice's laughter. She covered her ears to drown the sound out, but it didn't work. The laughter only became louder, and she couldn't tolerate it.

"STOP IT! STOP! STOP!" Meeka cried out, but that didn't help. Justice had full control of her mind right now, and Meeka knew Justice was enjoying every minute of it.

Meeka dropped to her knees and back paddled to the back of the shower. In her mind, the water was red and resembled blood. She stared at her body and blood was covering her like a jacket. She attempted to wipe the blood off, but it only made more blood on her body. Meeka stared at her body, and she was confused. She wasn't sure if it was actual blood or if her mind was playing tricks on her.

"I'm sorry Justice. I'm so SORRY! You made me do this to you. You basically pulled the trigger. I couldn't leave Izzy and Brink because of you." Meeka sobbed harder and dropped her head in her lap. She rocked side to side trying to comfort herself.

Hustle reentered the bathroom with a nightgown in his hand and smiling. When he noticed Meeka was crying and sitting on the shower floor, his smile faded away. He dropped the nightgown on the sink and grabbed a big blue dry towel. He rushed to turn the shower off and asked, "Tameeka, what's wrong with you baby?"

"I can't get it off me! HELP ME!"

"You can't get what off you?" Hustle covered Meeka's body with the towel and carried her out of the bathroom. He placed her on the bed and wiped her body off.

Meeka wiped her nose and said, "What if she was taking my side Brink? I took her life for no reason!!"

"It's okay Tameeka. Everything is going to be okay." Hustle said.

Meeka began to breath short and fast. Pressure sat on the center of her chest, and it felt like her chest was caving in. Once again, sweat was forming all over her body.

"Brink, I can't breathe. I think I'm having a heart attack. Oh my God no," Meeka deeply exhaled and held her chest tighter. They weren't sure what was going on, but Hustle needed to get Meeka to a hospital fast.

***

Meeka laid comfortably in the bed while eating a bowl of fruit cocktail. Two hours later she was stable, calm, and thinking in her right mind.

Hustle sat next to the bed with Isabella lying across his chest. Sydney sat at the edge of the bed eating a bag of Skittles and watching television. Her boys laid on the couch sleeping their little lives away. They didn't know it yet, but they wouldn't be attending school. Neither was Sydney, she had to be by Meeka's side. It didn't matter if it was a serious hospital stay or not, Meeka needed her.

"Meeka do you still have your membership at the gym?" Sydney asked.

"Yea, but I haven't been all month. Look at my gut, it's starting to show," Meeka pointed at her stomach and rolled her eyes. Hustle gave Meeka a stale frown and grabbed her stomach. Besides a little fat around her hips, Meeka's body was perfect from head to toe. Too bad Meeka didn't see it that way, and nothing could change her mind.

"It's starting to show where Tameeka? I don't see a thing wrong with your body." Hustle said.

"Of course you're going to say that Brink, you're my man."

"Girl that doesn't mean anything. When I gained those twenty pounds after Austin, and I got married he let me know asap. Ugh, just saying his name gives me the creeps."

"Seeing him when I was leaving his mom's house made my stomach turn. He's getting so small that it almost looks like he's smoking work." Meeka said.

"It really wouldn't surprise me, Meek. With the mind frame, he's in nowadays, smoking fits his personality. Thank God he's been staying his distance from us. When you go to the gym, you might run into him. You know majority of the police force works out at Cajun Fitness."

"That's the reason why I haven't been there all month. With all the drama that's attached to my name, they might arrest me there." She laughed.

"Right," Sydney laughed.

"Until all this clears up, I'll get some Denise Austin workout videos or something."

"You don't need to order workout DVDs. Just wake up in the middle of that night and workout with the infomercials." Sydney laughed.

"I think that's what I'm going to start doing and cancel my membership at Cajun Fitness." Meeka chuckled.

"Hell yea, it's only right. Have you seen the infomercial when this guy is doing the hip-hop dancing?" Sydney asked.

"Yea and he looks gay doing that shit. Talking about working out the abs, that's funny." Meeka chuckled. Sydney tried making conversation with Meeka, but she kept it short. The hospital wasn't somewhere Meeka wanted to be at 5:00 a.m., but she didn't have a choice. Her eyes were heavy, but she couldn't get much sleep.

"Are you feeling any better baby?" Hustle asked.

"A little bit, but I'm sleepy." She yawned.

"Well, you need to get some rest baby. You'll be here until tomorrow so get comfortable."

"I know, but this is weird. I'm in the same room Santana was in when he was in the hospital. I thought that would be the last time I saw this place. Boy was I wrong. I was wrong big time." Meeka stared at the ceiling, floor, and walls thinking of Santana. She closed her eyes for a second, and she could hear Santana talking and laughing in a low tone. The familiar and comforting sound warmed her soul.

"I miss that fool. I can't even front." Hustle laughed and shook his head.

"You aren't the only one Brink. The boys ask about him every day. No one could EVER replace him. That boy had a heart full of gold. I just hate how people judged him because he was a homosexual. All he wanted to be was accepted for who he was and loved. Unfortunately, he fell for the wrong person." Sydney dropped her head and sighed. She still couldn't believe that Santana was dead and she probably would never accept it.

"I still can't believe he's dead. The entire time Austin and Philly were plotting against my boy Tana. Have you spoken to his mom lately?" Hustle asked.

"Yea and she's still taking his death pretty hard. I can only imagine what it feels like to lose a child." Sydney said.

"Right and I'm sure she has guilt weighing on her shoulders as well. I hope I never have to experience losing a child. I bet that's a pain on a different level." Meeka said.

"When those guys jumped Santana, he still didn't let that bring him down," Sydney smirked and traveled through her thoughts…

Meeka, Justice, and Sydney all sat quietly in Santana's hospital room. No one said anything, and the tension was thick. Everyone knew who got Santana robbed, but to keep the peace Sydney and Meeka wasn't going to say anything.

Sydney sat next to Santana's bed crying. Santana's body was pretty bruised, but the doctors said that he would make a full recovery. Meeka knew it wasn't the time or place for it, but she wanted to explode on Justice. She knew Justice didn't have anything to do with it, but Austin's name was written all over it.

"Santana do you want some water or anything?" Sydney rubbed his hand and asked. He adjusted himself in the bed and said, "No, I'm good, but thank you."

"Are you sure Santana? I can run to Burger King and get you some breakfast. You know it's not a problem, just say the word." Meeka said.

"Y'all, I'm a little beaten up, but I'm not dead. I don't want anything, but to relax myself."

"Okay, but when you do just let us know," Sydney said.

"Trust me, before I can say anything I'm pretty sure y'all ask."

"I'm just glad you are okay. Did you recognize any of the guys? You said that it was three right?" Meeka asked.

"It was three guys that attacked me, but there was a driver. They were in a Camry, but I'm not sure about the color. Maybe it was black, but it could have been blue. It was dark outside, and I really couldn't tell. One of the guys said the name Hen."

"Hen, who the hell is Hen?" Justice asked.

"One guy had a tattoo on his left hand," Santana said.

"Are you sure?" Sydney asked.

"Trust me, I'm sure. How could I not see the fist that was coming toward my face?"

"Hen... Hen, wait a minute Hen as in Henry St. Patrick from Lawtell? His baby momma Jill drives a black Camry. You remember Jill, Santana? She was in our 3rd-grade class."

"Oh yea, I do remember her. Wasn't we in the 7th grade with her also, but she transferred to another school?" Santana asked.

"Yep, that's her. Now that's what you call a pill-popping animal. I once saw her chew a Lortab." The thought of someone chewing a chalky white pill made Meeka quiver and gag.

"It takes a pill popper to know one." Santana tried to laugh, but he held his left rib cage and moaned. Sydney covered her mouth and ran out of the hospital room. Meeka could hear her crying, so she ran after her.

She found Sydney sitting on the floor with her hands covering her face. Meeka sighed and dropped to the floor. She gave Sydney a hug and rubbed her shoulder.

"He's going to be okay Syd. You know Tana is a strong man and woman." Meeka laughed.

"He could have died or gotten severely hurt. I know Austin had something to do with this. This is my damn fault, just admit it."

"Don't say that Syd, this is not your fault. We just need to handle Austin before he makes another move."

"How are we going to do that?"

"That's easy, with a bullet." Meeka laughed, but Sydney didn't. Her tears rushed out, and she sobbed harder. Meeka exhaled and gave Sydney a hug. She hated that Sydney felt like it was her fault, but nothing Meeka said could change that.

"It's not funny Meek, none of this is funny. First Austin sends the police to my job, and then he gets Santana robbed and jumped. Who's next Meeka, you?"

"Don't think like that Sydney!" Meeka shouted and massaged her temples.

"How can I not think like that? Do you see how Santana LOOKS!!!!!!?? Santana is a solid 260 pounds, and they still managed to do him dirty. Just imagine what they would do to us! We're a 140 pounds a-piece. If they would stomp us, we would die."

"Now you're thinking and talking crazy. NOTHING WILL happen to us!"

"Yea you said that twice already and look what happened. Austin is playing with my job and Santana's life! Meeka, you didn't see the look in his eyes like I did. He's serious about putting us in jail. That's including Justice as well. Our next move has to be a serious move. It also has to be a move that will lead to our last move."

"What exactly are you saying, Syd?"

"I'm saying... I want out soon Tameeka." Sydney said.

"WHAT DO YOU MEAN YOU WANT OUT?!"

"Just what I said, I want out of this, all of this. I'm done with this lifestyle. I have kids to raise Tameeka, and I can't raise them from prison. If I go to jail, Austin will get custody of Tyric, Omari, Lana, and Angel. I can't let that happen, and I WON'T let that happen."

"What about teaching? You love those students, and that's the whole reason why you never wanted to escort full time."

"You know I love my students, but I can always teach somewhere else. I'm pretty sure my new students will love me the same, if not more. I really can't live like this anymore. Be honest Meek, we're getting too old for this shit."

"I really can't believe you're saying this. I would expect this from Justice or maybe even Santana. Not you Syd, not at all. This shit is what built us to be the women we are, but you're ready to give all that up?"

"The same shit that built us is going to slowly tear us down. Please, Meeka, I'm literally begging you, don't be stupid. Hustle is right it's time to get out of the game. I have to go, I'll call you later."

"Aiight." Sydney walked away and disappeared down the hall. Sydney said a mouth full, but Meeka wasn't sure how to process everything.

She paced back and forth down the hall thinking. She wasn't thinking about the things Sydney said. She was already plotting on getting Henry. "Oh yea Henry, I can't wait until I get you." Meeka laughed.

She stared down the hall and spotted Hustle talking to a nurse. The nurse pointed down the hall, but Meeka was already waving at Hustle to grab his attention. He told the nurse thank you and jogged towards Meeka. She met him halfway down the hall and gave him a tight hug.

"Are you okay baby?" Hustle kissed the side of Meeka's forehead and rubbed her hair. She didn't want to admit it, but she was a little worried. She held back her tears and shook her head up and down.

"Yea, I'm good."

"What the hell happened?" Hustle asked.

"Santana was jumped and robbed while he was in Lafayette."

"What, where is he? Is he okay?"

"He's good, and he's in that room. They stole his purse and beat him up pretty bad. The doctor said he has a broken rib and a sprained ankle. He has a black eye and a busted lip. They knocked out his tooth, but I'll make him an appointment to get it fixed. Besides that, he's fine, thank God."

"That's good, that's crazy though. Do you think Austin had something to do with it?" Hustle asked.

"Hell yea I do. Tana gave us some good information, and I have a good idea who it was."

"Who baby, tell me right now so I can go handle it."

"It's a guy named Henry St. Patrick, and he's from Lawtell. His girlfriend Jill drives a black Camry. I think he hangs with some guys named Sims, Jack, and Peppa. If Henry is the guy, it's a wrap. I don't care where I spot him I'm rocking out on him."

"Are you sure you don't want me to handle it? You already have Austin on your back."

"Yea, I'm sure. Where is Isabella?" Meeka asked.

"She's with my mom. Do you want me to go and get her?" Hustle asked.

"NO, leave her there. I don't want her to see Santana like this. Tell your mom I'll be there to pick her up in a few."

"Okay, I want you to know something," Meeka pulled Hustle closer to her and gave him a big kiss. He was a little surprised at all of the affection Meeka was showing him, but he wasn't going to say anything. He wasn't sure how long the affection was going to last, but for now, he was going to enjoy every second of it.

"What's that baby?" He asked.

"I love you, and I'm going to work on my feelings more. I really don't want to lose you."

"I'm glad to hear that, and I love you too. Sometimes you can be so cold. I feel like I hardly know you sometimes."

"I know, I know, and I'm sorry. I promise I will do better okay?" Meeka batted her eyes at Hustle and smiled. He turned away and smiled. He couldn't resist her big brown eyes or smile.

"Okay baby, but I have to go. Call me when you're on your way home."

"I will see you later." Hustle kissed Meeka on the cheek and walked away.

Meeka quietly reentered Santana's room and sat next to his bed. Justice was lying on the couch sleeping while Santana watched TV. He slightly turned his head to Meeka and smiled. She tried to fight back her tears, but she couldn't fight them back any longer. Santana motioned for Meeka to sit on the bed. He wanted to give her a hug, but his body was in too much pain, and his medicine hadn't kicked in yet.

"Meeka why are you crying? I told you that I'm okay. You know I will cover these bruises and black eyes with some make-up." He laughed.

"I'm scared, Santana. I think for the first time in life. I'm actually scared of something, not someone because Austin doesn't scare me. It's the things that he can do that scares me, the lives that can be taken, the finances that are riding on my back, and the truth being exposed. Everything is riding on one PERSON." Meeka whispered. She didn't want Justice to hear her talking, especially if it was about her brother.

"You can't think like that Meeka. You have to think smart before it's too late."

"I never told you this, but when you were little, your mom would worry about you so much."

"Why?" Santana asked.

"Being the new gay Cuban kid in a black community wasn't easy, and she knew that. Your mom always knew you were gay. She was worried the kids would pick on you, but I told her don't worry about anything. I told her as long as you have me in your life no one would harm you. If your mom was talking to you, she would be so disappointed in me. This is the one time I have let her down. I'm sorry Santana, I swear I am."

"Tameeka, you have no reason to be sorry. This isn't your fault, shit happens. If you want to blame someone, blame Syd. She's the one who married his crazy ass and brought him into our circle." He chuckled.

"Look at you Santana, how can you laugh at a time like this?" Meeka wiped her face, but the tears didn't stop.

"I can laugh because I'm not dead Meek. You need to calm down and chill out. Once I'm discharged, we're going to finish what Austin started."

"Okay Santana, whatever you say. Have you spoken to Jamie?" Meeka asked.

"No, but I did call her. I didn't get an answer or a callback. I guess she's still mad at me, go figure."

"Oh well, forget her. You have other things to worry about right now."

"I know, but I'm worried about her," Santana said.

"Don't worry about her right now Tana. You need to worry about yourself, so you can get out of this hospital. I'm tired of this place already." Meeka chuckled and softly rubbed Santana's leg. Then she walked to the head of the bed and fluffed his pillow. For some reason, she was nervous as hell and couldn't stay still. Santana laughed and grabbed Meeka's hand.

"You need to calm down Meek. I keep telling you I'm okay, I'm not dead."

"I know, but I'm sensitive behind you."

"Have you spoken to Rocko and Kane yet?" Hustle asked.

"Not since they made it to the airport. I'm sure she's going to call me when they make it home." Meeka said.

"Oh okay, I know it's going to be a while before we see them again. That damn Jupiter and Spencer, I salute them for that shit."

"You know we can always go to Bora Bora." Meeka smiled.

"I'm glad you said that. I had that in mind." He laughed.

"We should leave now, so I don't have to stay here. I'm sick and tired of coming to this damn hospital. The nurses and doctors are going to think we're looking for a free high." Meeka tried to laugh, but the medication she was on had her drowsy.

"Xavier is calling, I'll be right back," Sydney tiptoed out of the room and closed the door. Isabella slowly opened her eyes and Hustle was there to greet her with a smile. She rubbed her eyes and blushed, it made Meeka smile.

"Mommy," Isabella whispered.

"Yes, it is sweet girl."

"Izzy, do you want some breakfast?" Hustle asked.

"Uh huh."

"Okay, we'll be right back baby. Do you want anything, orange juice, pancakes, or a biscuit?"

"Pancakes and orange juice will be fine. Thank you, baby."

"You're welcome." Hustle climbed to his feet and walked out of the room. Meeka rolled to her side and stared at the door. In her mind, she was waiting for Santana to walk through the door with a long wig on. A few tears filled her eyes, but she didn't wipe them away. She wanted to be in her emotions and grieve the death of her best friend.

On the contrary, the thought of Justice betraying her made her dip into her thoughts again…

Today Meeka and Justice were finally meeting up. Justice told Meeka how she was depressed about Santana and needed to get away for a while. Justice forgot to mention how she was working with her brother against her. She tried her best to meet Meeka at her house, but Meeka insisted they go out for lunch. She lied and told Justice she hired a new cleaning crew to clean her home.

While Justice was on the phone with someone, Meeka sat at the bar in Sombreros. She was also on the phone talking to Hustle.

"Where is she?" Hustle asked.

"She's outside on the phone. She said she was talking to her new friend." Meeka dipped a tortilla chip into the salsa then took a sip of her Coke.

"Do you believe that?" Hustle asked.

"Do you believe that the earth is flat?" Meeka chuckled. She turned around to see where Justice was. She was still on the phone, but she looked tense.

"Not at all, she's probably on the phone with Austin. Be careful what you say, baby. I'm sure that wire is sitting between her breasts probably the center of her flat ass chest." Hustle laughed.

"That explains why she has on a crew neck t-shirt. As long as I've known her, she has never wore a crew neck shirt." Meeka sucked her teeth and rolled her eyes.

"Not even to Santana's funeral." He laughed.

"Right, the bitch had a low-cut dress on. I have to go, she's coming back."

"Okay, I love you." Hustle said.

"I love you too." Meeka disconnected the call and slipped her phone into her bra. Justice walked to the bar jolly and with a big smile on her face.

"Did the bartender come back yet?" Justice sat on the stool and reached for the bowl of chips. She poured a little salsa on her chips and stuffed a chip in her mouth.

Meeka stared at Justice with hate in her eyes. She was so disgusted with her. Even the way she chewed made Meeka angry.

"No, she is getting our food."

"Oh good because I'm starving," Justice said.

"You and me both, I'm glad you finally decided to get out of the house. We were missing you girl, and you had us worried." As Justice dropped her head, Meeka stared at her chest. She could see the print of the wire, and she laughed.

"Yea, this is nice. We haven't been here in a while." Justice said.

"I know and tomorrow is their drink special. I think we should come back tomorrow."

"Baby you know I'm down. I could use a few drinks in my system." Justice laughed.

"You and me both," Meeka gave Justice a fake smile and raised her eyebrows. The short blonde hair waitress approached the bar with a big black tray on her shoulder. The Chimichangas, tamales, and fish tacos looked delicious. Justice was ready to grab the hot plates of the tray herself.

The waitress swiftly placed the plates in front of them and pulled two sets of utensils out of her apron. She set the utensils down and asked, "Do you ladies need anything else?"

"No, I'm good," Meeka said, and she unwrapped the utensils and dug her fork into the Chimichangas.

"I need some extra pico and sour cream," Justice said.

"Okay, I'll be right back." She said and walked away.

"So Tameeka, what's the next move? I know you're plotting to kill whoever killed Tana."

"What?" Meeka asked with a mouth full of food.

"When is the next killing Tameeka?" Meeka wanted to laugh, but she held it together. She knew Justice was saying her full name for a reason. She shook her head and swallowed the food she was chewing. Then she took a big gulp of her drink and wiped her mouth.

"I was thinking about taking Izzy to Disney World. Lord knows we're overdue for a vacation." Meeka said.

"Speaking of Florida, do you still have those escorts in Miami? Isn't one of their names Misha or something like that?"

"I sure hope a hurricane doesn't form during that time? I do not want to get stuck in Florida."

"With the way you trick those hoes down there, getting stuck might be a good thing." She laughed.

"I was thinking we should put new flowers on Santana's grave every month. Clean around the tombstone often, keep it clean, and shit you know." Meeka said.

"Of course, Santana would kill us if we didn't. You know he was a neat freak." She laughed.

"His mom didn't want any of his things, go figure. I decided to donate his wigs to the hospital for the cancer patients." Meeka reached for a taco and shoved half of it in her mouth.

"Aawww that was a kind gesture Meek, what are you going to do with his clothes? He had some badass outfits." Justice said.

"I know I'll give them to someone who's in need of clothes," Meeka said.

"With all that money you make from pimping you can buy those people clothes." She laughed.

"You should try some of these tacos. They are waaayyy better than mine, but don't tell Brink that." Meeka continued to eat and ignore Justice. Meeka could tell Justice was getting annoyed at how she was ignoring her questions and comments. She knew she couldn't say anything because Austin could easily twist her words.

"Yea, I hear you." Justice turned away and rolled her eyes. Meeka slightly laughed.

"I wish you could have really met Santana's cousin Joseline. She's a cool girl, and she reminds me a lot of him. Crazy, loud, and silly, I need to visit her soon in Florida."

"That's where the money is," Justice said.

"Do you remember when that AKA was teasing you about your clothes? I think that was your second semester in college right?"

"Yea....you punched her in the nose for me. I didn't even know your name or who you were. You've been having my back for a long time."

"I told you, you're the sister I never had and always wanted."

Meeka's phone began to vibrate, so she pulled it out of her bra. It was Roman, she was surprised. She hadn't spoken to him since the club, and it was rare when he called her.

"Who is that?" Justice asked and leaned to the side to get a better view of Meeka's phone screen. Meeka pretended she didn't see Justice looking and covered her phone. The text message on her screen was something serious. It was about Justice and Miami. Meeka knew it couldn't be anything good.

"It's Brink's mom, she needs a loaf of bread from the store. Ugh, she acts like I'm her child instead of Brink."

"You basically are her child. That lady loves you like you're her daughter. Does she know what you do right?"

"The only thing I do is take care of Isabella and her son. I'm pretty sure she knows that." Meeka laughed.

"She would be heartbroken if she knew Tameeka was a pimp."

"The only thing you can call Tameeka is a mother. I wouldn't call myself a pimp because I played her son a few times. You can call me a playa, but not a pimp. Aw man, she's calling, let me take this." Meeka took a bite of her taco then jogged outside. Roman was calling her phone non-stop, and it started to scare her. On the sixth call, she quickly slid her finger across the screen and said, "Hello?"

"Tameeka, where are you?" Roman asked.

"I'm at Sombreros with Justice. Why what's up, is something wrong? Meeka asked.

"We need to talk in person. I got some information you may want to see."

"Your text message said it's something about Miami and Justice."

"Yea, but you need to see this yourself. When can we meet up?" Roman asked.

"We can meet up in a few minutes. Where are you now?"

"I'm leaving the gas station, I'll be at home," Roman said.

"Okay, I'll see you then." As Meeka turned around and Justice was walking out of the door, she kind of startled Meeka.

"Meek, do you want another drink?" Justice asked.

"Uhh, yea, a Sprite please, that other drink taste watered down."

"Okay, but is something wrong? It looks like you saw a ghost," Justice asked.

"Yea, I saw Casper." Meeka laughed and walked into the building.

"Girl you're crazy, but seriously, is everything okay?" Justice asked.

"Yea, Brink's mom was giving me a damn grocery list. I have to go, girl, I'm sorry."

"It's all good Meek, I'll pass by later."

"Okay, I'll text you when I get home." Meeka reached into her pocket and handed Justice a twenty-dollar bill. Meeka gave Justice a hug and asked, "What's that in your shirt?"

"Oh, it's my bra. The mental wire is starting to pop out. Don't judge me or tell anyone." She awkwardly laughed.

"Baby it's time to buy some new bras. Matter of fact, when I go to Walmart, I'll buy them for you. Just send me your bra size. You know Linda is sending me to three different stores." Meeka said.

"Okay, thanks, girl," Justice said.

"I love you Juju."

"I-I love you too Meek." Meeka waved and walked away. The grin on her face was priceless. She knew telling Justice she loved her would mess with her head.

Chapter 2

Now that Meeka was back home and feeling like her normal self, she had to get back to her business. She was glad to be discharged at noon and not a minute later. The strip club was still closed and would remain that way for the next month. The raid was all over the news and the towns of Opelousas, Lafayette, Sunset, and the surrounding areas. Meeka was pissed and ready to kill someone, mainly the person who caused the raid. Each day the club was closed, she was losing at least $15,000. She didn't want to stress about it, but she hated losing out on money, especially when it was because of a stupid broad and a dumb decision.

"I swear Brink, I'm going to slap the dog shit out Vixen when I catch her," Meeka said as she grabbed her backpack and closed the car door. She and Hustle finally made it home. Hustle pulled his gray 501 Levi Jeans to his hips and shook his head. He opened the front door for Meeka, but he stopped and turned around. Meeka stared at Hustle with a confused look on her face. She was tired and ready to get into the house.

"Look Tameeka, take the L and let it go." He said.

"Man, saying take the L is like telling me fuck me. Are you saying fuck me Brink?" She asked. She stared at Hustle waiting for an answer. She hoped he wouldn't say yes because that wasn't the answer she wanted in return.

"If that's how you want to take it, that's cool. You know I don't sugarcoat shit for no one and not even my girl. Now let's get in the house it's hot out here before you piss me the fuck off and ruin the rest of my day." Hustle walked into the house and stood next to the door. Meeka wanted to say something, but she didn't. The way Hustle handled her turned her on in many ways. The only thing she did was nod and crack a smile.

"I love you more Brink." She laughed.

Vixen was out of bounds and had a lot of explaining to do to Meeka. Too bad she was dodging Meeka's calls and was nowhere in sight. She was ready to kill Vixen, but she shook that thought off. Vixen was a weak link, and she wasn't worth the bullets.

"Home sweet home my love," Hustle smiled as he closed the door.

Meeka smiled back and said, "Yes, I was tired of that hospital bed anyways." She walked into the kitchen, and a grabbed a bottle of water. She quickly unscrewed the top and swallowed a large amount of water. It felt like she hadn't drunk any water for days and wanted more. Meeka grabbed two more bottles of water and walked out of the kitchen. Hustle grabbed her by the waistline and kissed her lips. She started to blush and turned away.

"I get so weak in the knees, I can hardly speak." She joked.

"Yea, yea, yea, I know I don't make you feel like that anymore. Those days are long gone and in the past."

"Oh my God B, you really think that I don't love you? You still make me feel like a high school kid," Meeka smiled and kissed Hustle's lips. Sometimes he didn't know how to react to Meeka's kind words and affection. He often thought she was joking and didn't take her seriously.

"Do you mean that Tameeka, from the bottom of your heart?" Hustle asked.

"I mean that from the bottom of my heart and the tip of my toes. You're my baby, and I love you with every breath in me. I thought you knew that, but I guess not," Meeka frowned and turned away. After all of the years they have been together, she still had to prove her love to him. In the beginning of their relationship, she thought about giving up. Once she realized how much Hustle loved her, she was glad she didn't give up. Hustle didn't know it, but he had some kind of hold on Meeka, and she loved it. He was the only man who had her head over heels. Not even Roman gave her butterflies like Hustle did.

"I love you too baby."

"Thank you for sticking by me through all this, seeing that blood was….scary. For a second, I thought it was my time to go, and karma was coming for me first. I guess all the bad I did finally catch up with me."

"It doesn't matter how you look at it now. What's important is that you're home, feeling better, and thinking straight. Now let's go upstairs and get you in bed," Hustle grabbed Meeka's hand and lead her up the stairs. Once they made it upstairs, Hustle moved Meeka to the side and opened their bedroom door. The room was cold and smelled like fresh laundry. Meeka inhaled the scent and walked to her bed. She placed the bottles of water on her pillow and grabbed her remote control for the TV.

"I'm going to get Izzy and my mom in a few minutes."

"You mean just Izzy, right," Meeka slowly pulled the covers back and climbed into the bed. Hustle adjusted the covers over her body and sat next to Meeka on the bed. The doctor's orders were for Meeka to get plenty of bed rest for the next few days. She totally agreed with him and was going to enjoy being waited on by Hustle.

"No, I said it correctly. I'm going to get Isabella and my mom."

"Don't play games with me Brink, why mom?" Meeka asked.

"My mom as in your future mother in law," Hustle turned away and waited for the shouting and loud talking Meeka was going to do.

"Hustle!

"Tameeka!"

"Tell me you're lying. I can't deal with your mom right now, tomorrow, or next week. She talks more bullshit than me, and you know that! You know your mom hates my guts and everything I stand for, ugh!"

"Well once you get your shit together, you won't have to worry about that. She's going to love you like the daughter she never had. Once Austin is dead, you'll be done with all this bullshit, right?"

"Aww come on Brink, not with this shit right now."

"Why not? You said after you handle the Philly and Austin situation you were done with the game."

"I just don't feel like arguing about this right not. Having your mom here will be enough drama for me. I can't even enjoy my first day out of the hospital," Meeka dropped her face into the palm of her hands and groaned. She knew Mrs. Tori was coming here for one reason and it wasn't to help Hustle take care of her.

"Tameeka she's coming here to help me with you and Isabella. You know how my mom is, she loves to take care of and help people."

"She loves to take care of and help everyone expect me. Don't act like your mom is a sweet angel towards me," Meeka rolled her eyes and dramatically exhaled.

"Stop acting like my mom is the damn devil."

"Hey, I'm calling it how I see it," Meeka said.

Tori and Meeka didn't have much of a good relationship, but they respected each other because of Isabella and Brink. Tori was no fool to Meeka's lifestyle and regularly heard the rumors about her in the streets. In Tori's eyes, Meeka turned Hustle out and pulled him into a whole different world. A few times she tried to set up Hustle on a few blind dates, but he never agreed to it. He didn't care that his mom didn't like Meeka, but it was necessary she respected his relationship.

What made matters worse; Hustle was a mama's boy before Meeka came along. Meeka changed that quick and made Hustle become an independent man. His mom no longer had to wash and fold his laundry. Meeka thought she was doing his mother a favor, but that made her hate Meeka more.

"Tameeka I don't talk about your mom, so I would like it if you didn't talk about mines."

"Ummm, that's because you never met my mom stupid." She laughed.

"Whatever, but please be nice when she gets here. I don't want the bickering and back and forth between you two. Let's all get along like the happy family we are." Hustle suggested, but Meeka yawned and pretended to ignore Hustle. He climbed on top of her and said, "Baby, please do it for me." Meeka wanted to say hell no, but she couldn't resist Hustle's charming smile. She shook her head up and down, and Hustle smiled again.

"I knew there was some nice in that heart." He joked.

"A very small amount that's for you and Izzy. Your mom, not so much, but I'll be nice for the sake of you. She knows she's still on my shit list because of that little date she tried to set up with."

"Tameeka let it go, that was three years ago." He demanded.

"So what, she was out of line for that."

"Your father called me today," Tori said.

"Oh yea," Hustle wasn't interested in hearing anything about his father. They didn't have much of a relationship, and he was okay with that. As a child, Hustle has seen his father disrespect his mom in numerous ways.

From infidelities, mental abuse, and financial issues, his dad has done it all to his mom. Hustle has never respected his dad and or wanted to be in his presence. In the past two years, his reached out frequently to Hustle. Sometimes he gave in, but majority of the time he didn't. It was too late for the two of them to mend their damaged relationship.

"Why, he needs some money or something?" Hustle asked and chuckled.

"No, he said he wanted to talk to you. He's been calling your old number."

"Oh okay, don't give him my number. I'll call him later or something." Hustle said.

"Why not call him right now baby? I could be tripping, but something seemed...off about your father." Tori said.

"What do you mean off?"

"I'm not sure, and I don't want to make any assumptions about that man. When you call him maybe, you can ask him." Tori smiled.

"I'm not really concerned about why he seemed off. He could have been high or under the influence mom."

"I'm just saying Brink, you don't have to start talking crazy. I'm well aware of what your father does."

Tori wanted to say more, but she ended the conversation and Hustle was glad. After everything his father has done to his mother, she still defended him. They were separated, but never officially divorced. Brandon was a crack addict and finding her husband passed out in a drug house was the last straw ten years ago. Tori could deal with a cheater, but not a drug addict.

"Okay, mom, whatever you say."

Hustle and his mom sat at the table at the Prejean's restaurant laughing and talking. Every week Hustle took his mom out for lunch so he could spend time with her. Since he was busy with Tameeka, he hadn't spent a lot of time with her. Last week he canceled and Tori was pissed. He wanted to cancel this week, but she begged him not to.

"I was thinking mom, we should take a family trip."

"That would be nice, I could use some sun on this pale skin," Tori rubbed her arm and laughed. Hustle chuckled and took a bite of his hot gumbo. He was surprised that his mom easily agreed to the trip. Probably because he didn't mention Tameeka was coming along.

"I know Tameeka could use a nice little getaway after everything that has happened. I must admit, she's a strong girl and is pulling through," Two weeks ago, Meeka was in a three-way car wreck and experience a miscarriage. She was only thirteen weeks pregnant when she lost the baby, and it was a boy. Hustle was devastated, but Meeka held her emotions together as much as possible. She didn't want the miscarriage to take a toll on her, even though it already slightly did.

"Oh she's coming along with us, I thought you said family Brink??"

"Mom, Tameeka is family, stop acting like a bitch." He demanded.

"Brink, you better watch your mouth when you are speaking to me. How is the family, is that your cousin? Are you committing incest and you didn't tell me?" She implied.

"She's my girl and the mother of my deceased child. That is family in my eyes, no matter if you want to admit it or not. I don't plan on leaving her anytime soon. I'm going to marry her." He smiled, but his mom frowned.

"Marriage with her, that's funny son. Don't be silly or foolish. She is not marriage material."

"Was dad marriage material mom? With those six brothers and sisters, I have in other states?" Hustle's harsh words offended his mother, but they were the truth. He couldn't understand how his mom talked down on Meeka but still praised his father.

"That's different, and you know that."

"In your world, it's different ma, but in reality, it isn't. Tameeka is going through a lot right now, and you could at least be nice. How would you feel if you lost your baby? She doesn't have much family in Opelousas. The family she does have here she doesn't talk to." Hustle said.

"Hmmm, I wonder what she did to them,"

"They were money hungry, and SHE stopped talking to them, damn mom. The girl can't win with you. You won't even give her a chance."

"How is she doing by the way?" Tori rubbed her eyes and twirled her fork. Hustle frowned and grabbed his mom's hand. Some days she hated Meeka and other days she despised her. Hustle couldn't figure out why because in

his eyes Meeka was perfect. She had a few flaws, but that didn't take away from how perfect she was to him.

"I mean, she doing okay I guess. The only thing we can do is take it one day at a time." Hustle said. A slim woman approached the table with a huge smile on her face. She stared at Hustle as if she knew him all her life. Love filled her eyes, but Hustle didn't understand why.

Tori grabbed her hand and made her sit down. The girl didn't take her eyes off Hustle, but he ignored her anyway. He couldn't lie, the girl was beautiful, but she didn't compare to Tameeka. Therefore, she couldn't grab or hold his attention.

While Hustle wasn't paying her any attention, she adjusted her hair with her hands. Her straight brown hair stopped in the middle of her back, she pulled it over her shoulders. She wanted Hustle to see how luscious and smooth her hair is.

"Son, don't be rude, stop eating your food," Hustle exhaled and dropped his fork.

"Hi." He said.

"This is Daisy Ballard. Daisy, this is my son Brink." Daisy seemed eager to meet Hustle, but it wasn't a mutual feeling. This was the second time this month that his mom pulled this little stunt. Setting him up on blind dates wasn't okay since he had a crazy girlfriend. If Tameeka found out about this, shit would get ugly for everyone.

Daisy stood about five foot even with an oval-shaped face. Her big smile disguised her bucked teeth and her awkward big nose. Her dark skin smelled of cocoa butter and was scar free.

"What's up," Hustle nodded his head and took a sip of his Coke. He wanted to tell the girl to leave the table, but he knew his mom would get upset with him.

"Hi Brink, it's nice to finally meet you. Your mom has said a lot of great things about you," Daisy batted her slanted brown eyes and smiled. Then she pulled her chair out and sat across from Hustle. Daisy rubbed her leg against Hustle's leg, but he moved his legs. She brushed it off and continued to smile at him. Hustle felt a little uncomfortable with the way she was staring at him. He wanted to tell her to stop, but he didn't want to offend her.

"Oh really, did she tell you that I have a girlfriend?" Hustle asked.

"She told me you were involved with someone, but I can look past that. You never know what the future holds for us," Daisy reached for Hustle's hand, but he pulled away. With his hands locked on top of his head, he stared at his mom. She avoided making eye contact with Hustle by turning her attention to Daisy.

"If you're fine with me having a girlfriend that means you're a home wrecker. That's the correct term right mom? That's what you called the women dad slept with," Tori's smile slowly faded away and she turned her body towards Hustle. He waited for her to agree with him, but she didn't say anything. Her body language spoke for her instead. Her thin lips were pressed together tightly, and her eyes were stretched wide. Hustle wanted to burst into loud laughter.

Daisy was a little offended by Hustle's words, but that wasn't going to make her leave the table or give up. Daisy has had her eyes on Hustle since Tori showed her a *picture of him six months ago. She loved that he was tall, handsome, and a mama's boy. Daisy knew if she became close with Tori that would lead her to Hustle's heart.*

"Anyways Brink, Tori is a 5th-grade teacher. That means she loves kids, just like you do." Tori smiled.

"Oh, okay." Brink said.

"I also graduated from LSU in Shreveport, and I'm going back to get my Master's degree." She smiled.

"Oh okay. Mom I'm about to go. Don't worry about the check, it's already paid for," Hustle took one more bite of his gumbo and wiped the corners of his mouth. Tori stood to her feet and grabbed his arm.

"Brink why are you being so rude to Daisy? I did not raise you to act this way!"

"You didn't raise me to be a player either, so this is not right. You know I have a girlfriend, and you know how much I love her. Why would you let this girl think she stands a chance next to Tameeka?"

"Stop talking like that God damn girl is a saint!! She's a savage, and everyone knows that!"

"I'm not a savage Mrs. Tori, I'm a good girl."

"MOM!" Hustle shouted.

Meeka and Sydney approached the table ready to fight. Tori glanced at Meeka and gave her a petty wave. Meeka wanted jump across the table and slap Tori, but she had to remind herself that she was Hustle's mom.

"What the fuck is this?" Meeka pointed at everyone at the table waiting for answers. Meeka's chest expanded in

and out, she was furious. Tori sat at the table with a smirk on her face and Meeka wanted to slap it completely off. She loved pissing Meeka off, and she did it well. Daisy seemed afraid, and Meeka knew it wouldn't take much to make her exit the table. Hustle dropped his head and sat down. He wasn't surprised that Meeka showed up.

"It's a restaurant sweetheart. I'm sure you have been to one before." Tori's responded while laughing. Her laughing drove Meeka crazy. She wanted to grab Hustle's bowl of gumbo and toss it on Tori to make her shut up. Tori knew how to get under Meeka's skin, and she did it well.

"Mrs. Tori today will be the day! I'm getting sick and tired of your bullshit!"

"Tameeka watch your mouth!" Hustle shouted, and everyone in the restaurant stopped what they were doing. All of the attention was on the table, but no one seemed to care.

"NO Brink, tell her to watch her damn mouth! She's always getting in our relationship, and I'm sick of it. I'm sick and tired of this being a three-way relationship."

"Her, what do you mean her? I have a name little girl and its Tori."

"I DON'T CARE WHAT IT IS!!" Meeka shouted.

"Tameeka how did you know we were here?" Hustle asked. He seemed guilty, but he had nothing to hide.

"The bitch posted it on Facebook that she had a date with YOU," Sydney pulled her phone out of her pocket and showed Hustle the Facebook post. Hustle turned to

Daisy and shook his head. The smile and lustful look was
still on her face.

"Tameeka that's a lie, and I didn't know nothing
about this. My mom set this shit up. Please believe me." He
begged. Meeka glanced at Tori and flared her nose.

Meeka laughed silently at the memories and shook
her head. A lot of things changed since then.

"It's time for you to take your medicine baby,"
Hustle walked into the room with an Escitalopram pill in
his hand and holding a cup of orange juice. Meeka grabbed
the pill out of his hand and tossed the pill into her mouth.
Then she took a big gulp of the orange juice and swallowed
the pill. The orange juice was refreshing, but she didn't like
the bitter taste it left on her tongue.

"Ugh, no more of that cheap shit. We can afford
Sunny D." She laughed.

"Hey, the corner store was out of Sunny D, be
humble." He joked.

"I am baby."

"I'll be back and when I get back, PLEASE be on
your best behavior." He begged.

"Okay, but you should tell her the same thing." Meeka
rolled her eyes and Hustle did the same as he walked out of
the room. With every second that past, Meeka was dreading
Tori being in her home.

Meeka lied in bed bored out of her mind. Thirty
minutes had gone by, and Hustle still wasn't back at home.
She knew Tori had Hustle running a hundred errands. She
shuffled into her pocket for her phone to call Sydney, but

she changed her mind. She forgot Sydney was at work and couldn't answer any personal calls. She needed someone to vent to about Tori, but she had no one to talk to. At a time like this, she usually called Santana or Justice to fix her problems. Justice was the one who gave advice while Santana would make jokes out of the situation. Meeka hated that he wouldn't take anything seriously, but his humor always put her in a good mood. Ten minutes later, she could hear Hustle laughing, and her attitude shifted. Tori's laughter followed behind his, and it made her attitude shift again.

"Tameeka!" Hustle shouted.

"Ugh, here we go." She whispered.

"I'm coming, give me a second," Meeka rolled out of bed and rushed to her bedroom mirror. She pulled her purple fuzzy robe off and dropped it to the floor. With the tip of her fingers, she slicked her baby's hair down and tightened her high ponytail. She didn't look her best, but she was presentable.

"Baby, why are you taking so long?" He shouted again.

"I'm coming Brink," Meeka walked out of the room and rushed down the stairs. She spotted Isabella on the couching eating an ice cream cone and rushed to her. Isabella's smile grew bigger, and she began to laugh. Meeka squatted to the floor and gave her daughter a tight hug. It felt like she hadn't seen her in years.

"Awwww, I miss you, pretty girl."

"Well hello Tameeka," Tori said.

Without turning around, Meeka replied, "Hey Mrs. Tori how are you?" Meeka continued to hug Isabella because she didn't want to turn around. Hustle cleared his throat and discreetly kicked Meeka's leg. Meeka moved her leg and flared her nose. She slowly turned around and said, "Hi Mrs. Tori how are you today?"

"I'm fine, what about yourself?" She asked.

"I'm good, and I'm glad to be home from the hospital. Your son was Superman while I was there." She laughed.

"You know you're my baby, it's my job to take care of you," Hustle said as he grabbed Meeka by the arm and gave her a comforting hug. Meeka buried her face in his chest and enjoyed the hug. Hustle had loved all over her, but she could still feel his mother's eyes burning the back of her head. She wanted to mumble a few words to Hustle, but Meeka knew he would say she was tripping and overacting.

"The woman is supposed to take care of the man, not the other way around Brink," Tori said.

"Chill mom, that was back in the day. It's 2015, and we're doing things differently." He laughed.

"I take care of your son Mrs. Tori, very well actually." Meeka snapped, and Hustle nudged her.

She nudged him back, and he mumbled, "Don't start."

"Tell her the same thing. Clearly, you didn't have the talk with her." She whispered.

"Tameeka, when are you going to clean this place? I could smell the germs as soon as I stepped foot in the door. My grandbaby can't live like this sweetheart."

"Excuse me, she can't live like what?"

"Mom, really? Nothing is wrong with our house." Hustle implied.

"This is y'all's home now? I didn't know you two purchased this home together," Mrs. Tori sat on the couch and crossed her skinny legs. Meeka was ready to break them in half. Everyone knew Meeka purchased the home before she met Hustle, but that didn't mean it wasn't their home.

"Yes, it is and always has been that way." Hustle said.

"You want to know something Tameeka?" Tori asked.

"What's that?" Meeka snapped, but she calmed down. It seems like every word that came out of Tori's mouth pissed Meeka off. Even the way she sat on the couch with her nose in the air annoyed Meeka. She acts as if Meeka's two-story house was a project on the south side of town.

Tori looked around the living room as if she was disgusted. Meeka felt insulted and wanted to spazz out. She hadn't been home in a few days, but her home was spotless. As Tori shook her head, her bob haircut bounced freely, she was as stuck up as a person could get, but Meeka never understood why. She was the wife of a drug addict and the mother of a drug dealer.

"A maid three times a week would do this place some justice. They could also shampoo the carpets and sanitize the walls for you." She smiled.

"Mrs. Tori, my home is clean, and I don't 'smell' any germs. There isn't a stain on the walls or carpet. Maybe you're seeing things. Brink, you should take your mom to the eye doctor. I would hate for her vision to get worse than what it already is."

"Tameeka chill, please and thank you." Hustle interrupted.

"All I'm saying Tameeka is a little help wouldn't hurt you," Tori said.

"That's why I have your son he's all the help I need." Meeka gave Tori a fake smile and excused herself from the living room. Meeka could feel Tori's eyes following her, but she didn't care. She needed get out of Tori's presence fast and calm herself down.

Meeka walked into the kitchen and exhaled. She placed her opened hands on the countertop and dropped her head. She hated how she let Tori get the best of her, but she couldn't help it. Tori's a big part of Hustle's life, and Meeka knew Hustle hated his two favorite women feuding all the time. It didn't matter how many times Meeka tried to be the bigger person Tori always threw shots at her. Whether it was her hair, body weight, cooking, or cleaning, Meeka couldn't do anything right. No one knew it, but the real reason Meeka wasn't ready to marry Hustle was because of his mom. Over the years, Tori tried her best to damage their relationship. Meeka could only imagine the things she would do to end their marriage.

"I swear, this lady is the devil himself," Meeka softly banged her hands against the countertop and tossed her head backward. Then she turned her head to the left and stared at the half-empty bottle of Hennessy. She wanted to take a few sips, but she had to wait until Tori left. If she smelled the loud alcohol on Meeka's breath, she would quickly label her an alcoholic.

"Tameeka what did we talk about earlier?" Meeka rolled her eyes the second she heard Hustle's voice. His tone was firm and sharp, something she always hated.

She turned around and said, "Brink you need to talk to your mother. I am trying my best to not argue with her, but she's pushing all the right buttons!!! It doesn't matter what I say, she's going find something wrong with it. I'm starting to feel like she's in competition with me."

"What?" Hustle laughed.

"I think your mom is competing with me for you. What kind of incest shit yall have going on?" Meeka asked and laughed.

"Tameeka stop playing with me, my mom is not competing with you for me."

"Hmmmm, well it's something she wants, and it seems like I'm standing in her way," Meeka said.

"You're tripping, and you don't need to think like that. You are my woman, and that's it. I really want my woman and my woman to get along. Is that too much to ask for?"

"No baby, it's not, but you need to have this conversation with your mom. I don't have a problem with her. She has a problem with me. What I won't continue to allow is your mom disrespecting me in my home. That shit is not cool Brink, and you know that. I have the highest respect for your mom even though she treats me like shit. I don't go to her house and talk crazy to her!"

"That's because you never go inside." He laughed.

"I don't go inside because she doesn't want me inside of her house!! It's not funny Brink, and enough is enough. If your mom thinks she can continue to speak to me this way, I have a big news flash for her."

"Baby you need to calm yourself down and relax. You haven't been home for two hours, and I bet your blood pressure is through the roof. Let me handle my mom, and you be cool. The only thing YOU need to worry about is getting that beautiful face of yours back on track," Hustle stood behind Meeka and rubbed her shoulders. She moaned in a whispered and rolled her neck. The massage felt good, but it wasn't good enough to make her remember who was sitting in her living room.

"Why won't you see it just like me Brink? I haven't done anything wrong to your mom."

"Sssshhhhh and forget about her. I like you, and that's all that matters," Hustle slowly eased his hands down Meeka's back and landed on her ass cheeks. He squeezed and lifted her ass cheeks.

"Are you going to show me how much you like me tonight?" Meeka bit her bottom lip and used Hustle's hand to caress her vagina. He nibbled on her ear a little and nodded his head up and down.

"Yep, over and over I will." Hustle's touch always made Meeka weak, so she wanted to jump on top of him in the kitchen. She didn't care if his mom walked in and saw their naked bodies humping one another. Maybe she was frustrated with her own sex life.

"Maybe your mom is frustrated because she needs some dick in her life," Meeka laughed.

"I don't know, and I don't want to know about her sex life." He laughed.

"Maybe she wants a little throwback dick from your dad?" Meeka snickered, but Hustle squeezed her butt cheek. She jumped a little and massaged the area where the pain was.

"I highly doubt that, do you know how long it's been since my mom and dad have been together?" Hustle asked.

"How long?" Meeka asked.

"Too damn long Tameeka, ugh, that would be disgusting. After sex, he probably would pull his drugs out and offer my mom some. That would be the day he would be on a t-shirt, and I would be on the news."

"You're saying all of that, but isn't it weird how your mom never divorced your dad?"

"What do you mean?" Hustle pulled his hands off of Meeka's ass and stood next to her. Meeka grabbed a banana out of the fruit bowl and began to peel it. Then she took a big bite and thoroughly chewed it. Hustle grabbed the banana and took a bite as well.

Meeka cleared her throat and said, "It's kind of weird how your mom didn't divorce your dad. That's because she still wants to be with him."

"Ha, ha, ha, that's hilarious Tameeka. Everyone knows my mom hates my dad." Hustle said.

"Yea, she hates him soooo much, but she's always in contact with him. Don't be a fool baby, you're smarter than that."

"Oh forget that. I forgot I have something to show you."

"What is it, baby?" Meeka asked. Hustle pulled his phone out of his pocket and unlocked the screen. He quickly scrolled through his pictures and handed Tameeka his phone. She stared at the house and said, "That's a nice house, but whose is it?" She asked.

"If these two buyers back down, it could be ours." Hustle smiled.

"Really, where is this house?" Meeka asked.

"It's in San Diego, sunny San Diego."

"As in San Diego, California?" Meeka asked.

"Yea, that's the only San Diego I know of." He laughed.

"Why are you looking at houses out there and we live here?"

"Once you wrap this bullshit up, that's going to be our new home."

"Wrap what shit up?"

"Come on Tameeka don't play dumb, we made an agreement. I gave you a time frame, and you agreed to it." Hustle implied.

"Uhh yea, I did agree to it, but is Austin dead?" She whispered.

"No, he isn't, but hurry that shit up. By the time you clear that lil' business up this house or another house should be available. I saw two other houses for a little cheaper, but I have my eyes on this one. The realtor sent me pictures of the backyard, and it's huge, it's bigger than the backyard we have now. The house is in a quiet neighborhood with a great private school district. We'll never hear gunshots and drunks arguing again." He laughed.

"You already spoke to a realtor?" Meeka asked. She was a little surprised at how fast Hustle was moving. She secretly didn't want to move or get out the game, but time was winding down. Hustle had everything figured out while Meeka was still back paddling to her old money.

"Well yea, Mike is keeping in contact with me every day. You do want this right? I gave you enough time to get it together, right?"

"Yea, you did. I'm home, and that should tell you something." Meeka's heart was racing, and she would tell Hustle anything to get him off her back. By the way, Hustle was speaking she knew he thought she was completely out of the game.

"So, no more strip club?" Hustle asked.

"No, no more He He's. I'm not sure when they are reopening it anyways. I told you I don't want to lose you or

Isabella, I love you, baby," Meeka grabbed Hustle by his belt loops on his jeans and pulled him closer to him. From the lies she was fluently telling, her heart was racing. She hated lying to Hustle, but right now, that was her only option.

"I love you more Tameeka, believe that. I can't wait to see you running butt ass naked through our new house. Ass and breast will be swinging everywhere," Hustle grabbed Tameeka's ass again and laughed. When he heard his mom's footsteps approaching the kitchen, he removed his hands.

"Brink, can you run to the store and get me a coke?"

"No need to mom, there are Cokes in the fridge," Hustle walked to the icebox and pulled the door handle. He scanned the crowded icebox for the bottle of Coke, but his mom stopped him. He turned around, and she said, "Uuhhh, no baby, I rather one from the store if you don't mind."

"What's the difference Tori, it's the same drink?" Meeka asked.

"It's no problem mom, I'll be right back."

"Yea, we know Brink," Meeka walked out of the kitchen and held her composure together. She knew the real reason Tori wanted a drink from the store and not out of her home. Tori never ate a thing out of the house which was another insult to Meeka. Hustle tried to kiss Meeka before he walked out of the door, but she turned away. Hustle frowned, but he didn't say anything. He didn't want to make a scene in front of his mom, so he kissed Meeka on the cheek and walked out of the door.

Tori walked into the living room and sat across from Meeka. Meeka kept her eyes on the television because she didn't want to make eye contact with Tori.

"If you don't mind, I put Isabella down for her nap," Tori said.

"No, I don't mind, thank you," Meeka replied.

"That little girl is growing by the second and looking likes Brink's twin." She smiled.

"She is and before I know it she'll be dating little boys. I'm definitely not ready for that and the heartbreaks that are going to come with."

"All I can tell you is take it one day at a time. Until then, enjoy her while she's still young." Tori replied.

"I am." Meeka wasn't in the mood to talk to Tori and wanted to keep her replies direct and short. She wasn't sure if Tori was just making conversation or being a normal mother in law.

"Brink showed me the pictures of the house he wants to get for you guys," Tori said.

"Yea, it's a beautiful home," Meeka said.

"Since you guys are moving that means you are starting a new chapter in your life?" Tori asked and smiled.

"What does a new chapter mean?"

"Like being a better mother and working a regular job."

"Hold up a second, you can make comments about how I make my money. What you will not do is EVER make a comment about my parenting. If I'm not good at anything else, I'm good at being a mom to my daughter. Isabella is the best thing that has happened to me, and I give her the world."

"Okay Tameeka, you don't have to get so defensive. I'm only speaking my mind and telling you how I feel. You could take a few parenting skills from me." She chuckled.

"Why would I take advice from you when your son has been selling drugs since he was a kid? He's in his thirties now, so you do the math. You are separated from your husband, but is still legally married to him." Meeka snapped.

"My son chose to sell drugs. He could have gotten a job just like the rest of the boys in the neighborhood. Besides that, what does my marriage has to do with parenting? You and my son have been together for a while, but he still hasn't married you! I'm sure you are the problem because my Brink is perfect."

"NO, YOUR BRINK IS NOT PERFECT SO YOU CAN GET THAT STUPID SHIT OUT OF YOUR HEAD!"

"Excuse me, who the heck are you talking to like that?" Tori shouted.

"I'm sure you heard the saying that no one is perfect. The reason why we aren't married is because of YOU! I know you would try everything in your power to make him divorce me. From day one you hated me and never took the opportunity to get to know me."

"I don't need to get to know you Tameeka. I know enough about you. I am not pleased with what I know, but I tolerate you because of my son and granddaughter."

"See Tori, this is the bright side of the situation, you don't HAVE to tolerate me."

"That's good, and this is the first time we agree on something," Tori said.

"Mrs. Tori, why do you hate me so much? I'm nothing, but nice to you and your son, but you treat me like shit. When Brink and I first got together, I wanted you to like me so much. I went above AND beyond to be on your good side, but you didn't acknowledge that. I thought you would fill the motherless void in my life and we would have a strong bond. I was wrong, and I'm okay with that. I no longer care about any of that or being on your good side. I love your son, and he loves me as well. We're going to be together forever, so you have to accept and deal with that. If you don't, so be it, life will go on."

"You are no good for my son and one day he'll see it."

"I'm starting to see that you are no good for him either. Maybe he'll see that as well, and maybe that's why your husband cheated so much."

"Watch…your…damn….mouth! You don't know anything about my husband or marriage."

"Just like you said, I know enough. Now get the fuck out of my house before I throw you out!" Meeka jumped to her feet and walked to the front door. Tori could see the anger in Meeka's eyes, so she grabbed her purse and stood to her feet.

As Meeka opened the door, Hustle was doing the same thing. Tori locked eyes with his mom and said, "Who started it?"

"She did as usual, and this time, I finished it. Like I said Tori, get the hell out of my house!" Meeka sized up Tori and walked away. Meeka was waiting on Tori to leave so that she can have round two with Hustle.

"Tameeka, mom, what the hell is going on?" Hustle tried to hand his mom the cold Coke he brought for her, but she declined it and continued walking. Meeka ran up the stairs leaving Hustle in the middle of the living room confused. He wasn't sure what direction to run in, but he decided to chase after Meeka.

He entered his bedroom and found Meeka sitting at the edge of the bed. Tears flowed down her cheeks, and her sobbing was low. Hustle hadn't seen Meeka cry like this since she was told Santana was dead.

"What happened and why are you crying?" Hustle asked.

"Brink just go, I don't want to talk about it," Meeka wiggle the hair away from her wet face and wiped her nose. Hustle walked to the edge of the bed, but Meeka stood to her feet and walked to the bathroom. Hustle sighed and followed behind her even though she said she didn't want to talk about it.

"No, I'm not leaving so tell me what the problem is."

"There is no problem anymore, I finally fixed that shit." Meeka laughed.

"Tameeka what the hell are you talking about and what is the problem?"

"Stop screaming in this house before you wake Isabella up!" She grunted. Even though she told Hustle, not to hell, she still spoke loudly. She didn't like arguing while Isabella was home, but she couldn't control her emotions. Tori unleashed a truckload of emotions Meeka had hidden for years, which was not having a mother in her life.

"You're also screaming Tameeka! Maybe you should take your own advice as well."

"YOUR MOM BRINK, I HATE HER WITH A PASSION. I HATE THAT WOMAN WITH EVERY BONE IN ME!! SHE TELLS ME THAT I'M NO GOOD FOR YOU, AND ONE DAY YOU'LL SEE THAT. WHO IS SHE TO TELL ME I'M NO GOOD FOR YOU BRINK? WHO MADE YOUR MOTHER THE COMMANDER TO JUDGE ME?!"

"Baby you need to calm down and stop letting my mom get under your skin. You've been dealing with her for years, so why are you letting her get to you now? You know she's only talking shit, and it's going through one ear and out the other."

"See Brink, that's the problem. I've been dealing with her ass for years. I'm tired of it, and I can't deal with this anymore. All your mom do is bring me down when she's around. She makes me feel like a piece of shit, and I am not a piece of shit Brink!! I am a good person, and I KNOW I'M A GOOD PERSON!!" Meeka wanted to stop crying, but her tears had a mind of their own. The more she thought about Tori's hurtful words and her mother's absence, her heart ached. She was done pretending she was tough and hiding how she felt.

"I think you need to lie down and relax, you had a long week. You're overreacting to this bullshit, and I don't like seeing you like this," Hustle grabbed Meeka and gave her a bear hug. The tighter he hugged her, the more she cried.

Hustle hadn't seen Meeka this emotional in a while, and he was puzzled. He always knew the strong woman who didn't let much bother her. He never thought the arguments with his mom bothered her so much and he hated how blind he was to it.

"I don't want to lie down Brink. I want to stop feeling like this. I want this feeling to go away and to never come back."

"You want to stop feeling like what?"

"I want to stop feeling like I'm a total fuck up and a waste of your time. I feel like I'm a waste of everyone's time Brink. I try my best to be a great woman, but somehow I always fall."

"Tameeka stop that. You are a fantastic woman. If you weren't fantastic, I wouldn't be with you." He chuckled.

"I'm serious Brink. You can have any woman you want so why are you still wasting time with me?" Meeka asked.

"Now you're talking crazy. I haven't wasted any time with you. From the day we met, I knew you were the one for me. I thought about proposing right then and there, but that would have been creepy." He laughed.

"Are you serious?"

"If Pedro was here, he would tell you that. I told him how I can tell you were my soul mate and he laughed. He said I was corny as hell, but that's what I felt in my heart. After everything we have been through, the good and the bad, we are still together. Neither one of us is perfect, but I love the hell out of you. Everything about you makes me love you more every day. Forget what my mom is saying about you, I love you, and that's what matters."

"I love you too baby, but with your mom being the way she is, this won't last much longer. I can't continue to argue with her, and I won't make you choose between me and her. That's your mother, but I don't have a soft spot for her. I guess it's because I don't have a mother of my own or maybe because I don't like your mom."

"I didn't know it bothered you this much, I'm sorry. I hate seeing you cry like this, that shit fucks with my head. A pretty face like yours only deserves smiles, nothing less. My mom, on the other hand, I'm going to handle that shit."

"Are you serious?" Meeka asked.

"Yea, I am. I can't have anyone speaking to my woman any kind of way. If I knew this bothered you so much, I would have checked it a long time ago."

"Brink, how could you not tell it bothered me? Your mom says some hurtful things to me. My mom was a good woman, and she would have never spoken to you the way your mom speaks to me. I thought your mom would have been my mom as well. Boy was I wrong. That was like a stab in the heart," Meeka shook her head and turned away.

"So, that's what it's all about my mom or your mom?" Hustle asked.

"I guess it is about that. When I was growing up, all I had was Santana and Marlo, and they had me. Since Santana was gay and always dressed like a woman, I sometimes looked at him as a mother." Meeka said.

"Are you serious?" Hustle asked.

"Yea I'm serious. From the day my mom died, I craved to have a mom in my life. I wanted a mom like the ones you see in movies and television shows, a perfect mom. When I was at school, I would see all the other kids with their moms, and it would hurt. I would sneak off to the restroom and cry. Some days I would cry for hours and beg God to send me a mom, but he never did. After a while, I stopped begging and stopped talking to God, and suddenly the tears stopped as well. The one time he did spend a mom, she was terrible. I never understood why I had to go through life wanting someone so badly."

"Tameeka its okay, nothing is wrong with you wanting a mom. I wanted my dad there, but that didn't stop him from doing drugs or cheating on my mom. I would beg my dad to stop, but he wouldn't. At one point, I think my dad cheated because it gave him a high. I also think that once that high was gone, he searched for something else and turned to drugs. I tried talking to my mom about it, but she always changed the subject. She could never handle the truth about my father." Hustle said.

"Brink, she basically called me a bad mom. Me, a bad mom, can you believe she said that?" Meeka asked and shook her head. Hustle rubbed the back of his neck and shook his head from side to side.

"No baby, you are not a bad mom."

"I know I'm not the world's best mom, but Brink I love Isabella with eeevvvveerryyyyythhhhiinnngggg that is in me! I would take a bullet for her and give her my last breath because I love her dearly. When I found out that I was pregnant, I told myself I would be the best mom I could be and I would give my baby all the love that is possible to give. The way Izzy looks at me tells me a lot. I know she thinks I'm the world's best mommy." Meeka laughed.

"You are Tameeka, and no one can tell her different. You have enough going on in your life, and I don't want you to stress because of this." Hustled said as Tori walked into the room, but Meeka gave her a dirty look. She fumbled with her fingers and Meeka could tell she was nervous. After all the shit she just talked, Meeka didn't understand why Tori was acting nervous and couldn't stand still.

"Didn't I tell you get out of my house?"

"I know Tameeka, and I want to say something before I leave. If you still feel the same way I totally understand and I will never come back." Tori replied.

"What is it?" Meeka asked.

"I'm sorry, I'm so sorry for everything I have said and done to you. You've made bad decisions in life, but we all have. That doesn't make you a bad person. I have done things I'm not proud of, and I have no reason to judge you. I honestly don't think you are a bad person. Brink is always saying great things about you and Isabella loves you dearly. I can see it in her eyes every time she looks at you."

"Okay, if you feel like that, why do you hate me so much?" Meeka asked.

"I don't hate you, hate is a strong word," Tori said.

"Hate IS a strong word, and that's exactly how I feel. I feel like you hate me just like these people in the streets do. I'm not hurting your son nor will I ever hurt your son. I'm only doing what I need to do to survive. I never want Isabella to grow up the way I did or do the things I did. I want her to be so scared of drugs and the streets that she thinks cigarettes are a drug."

"Answer the question mom, what stupid ass reason do you have for hating Meeka? It's time to put it all on the table for once and for all. I'm tired of being in the middle of this, it's childish and stupid." Hustle said.

"Please Mrs. Tori, tell me why. I need to know why you hate me like an enemy. I am basically your daughter in law, a piece of signed paper can't make Brink and I closer."

"Your high light skin and long hair makes me dislike you," Tori said.

"What?" Meeka and Hustle both asked. Meeka was shocked at Tori's response, and Hustle didn't know what to think. Tori's a beautiful dark chocolate woman with kinky soft brown hair. Because of her high cheekbones and full top lip, Meeka always compared her to Naomi Campbell. Her head was always in the air when she walked, and some would say she thought her shit didn't stink. Tori graduated from Southern University and pledged Alpha Kappa Alpha sorority. She took pride in her sorority and wore her colors and pearls proudly.

"Mom are you serious?" Hustle asked.

"I'm embarrassed to admit it, but yes, I'm very serious."

"I always thought you hated me because you felt like I was pulling Brink away from you. I never thought it was become of the way I look. Wow, that's crazy Mrs. Tori. I can't control the way I look."

"I know you can't control that Tameeka and not only because of how you look. Every woman my husband cheated on me with looked like you. None of the women were darker than Brink or Isabella. All of them had shoulder length hair or longer. That man had a fetish for light skin women, and it made him sick to my stomach. It made me feel like my skin tone wasn't beautiful and that was the reason why I couldn't keep him. I'm not sure if I ever had Brink Senior to myself, he was always creeping on me."

"I – I – I don't know what to say, I'm speechless. I've always seen you as this beautiful and gracious woman. You wear your pink, green, and pearls with pride. You're the reason I wanted to enroll into college and pledge AKA. We all know that school junk isn't for me. It's not a time that you have walked into a room, and all eyes weren't on you. If I can get the respect you do, I would be a better woman and role model."

"Isabella is light skin with long hair as well, do you hate my daughter?" Hustle asked. Meeka could see he was getting angry and she was afraid of what he would do to his mother. She slowly approached him and grabbed his hands.

"Brink, calm down," Meeka whispered, but she kept a smile on her face. She didn't want Tori to see that she was nervous. It was hard to disguise the shaking her hands were doing.

"Calm down my ass! Mom, do you hate my daughter and I want to know the truth?"

"Brink, can you please sit down and calm down. I don't like the way you look, and you're scaring me." Tori begged, but that didn't change Hustle's demeanor.

"I'm not going to sit down. TELL ME THE GOT DAMN TRUTH MOM!!"

"Okay, okay, at first I didn't. She looked exactly like Tameeka and made me feel the pain your father made me feel. I'm sorry Brink, I'm so sorry." Tori said.

"Mom, Isabella is a child, and you hated her because of something petty. I can't believe this. I thought you were better than that. Wait a minute, have you ever hurt her? I swear to God mom if you laid a finger on my child I will…"

"BRINK, STOP! THAT IS STILL YOUR MOTHER! You need to calm down before you react in a terrible way," Meeka said before Hustle could raise his hand in mid-air Meeka grabbed it. She stood in front of him and pinned his arms against his legs. In fear and with eyes full of tears, Tori rushed out of the room. This time Hustle didn't chase behind his mom.

"I can't deal with this shit anymore," Hustle wiggled his arms out of Meeka's grip and walked to his bed. Then he kicked his shoes off and laid across their big bed.

Meeka's thoughts were everywhere, and she couldn't think straight. She stood in the middle of the room, but she didn't say anything. After everything Tori said, she didn't have much to say.

"You can officially say the cat has my tongue. Your mom hates me because of something I don't have control over. She doesn't hate me because of you. I'm not sure how to feel about that. I would rather her hate me because of you. This is some crazy shit." Meeka buried her wide face into the palm of her hands and laughed. She wasn't laughing because it was funny. Meeka was laughing because she finally found a woman who was just as crazy as her.

***

Today was a cool, but sunny day in Opelousas. The temperature sat in the high 70's which allowed the kids in the neighborhood to enjoy the weather. Isabella was out with Sydney and Hustle was running errands for Meeka. No one had spoken to Tori since the big argument, and Meeka wasn't sure how to feel about that. Her days were peaceful, and she wasn't in any mood to argue with Hustle or his mother. She wanted Hustle to apology to his mother for the way he disrespected her, but Hustle told her no. If anyone should be apologizing over and over, it should be Tori. For the time, Hustle didn't want Tori in the presence of him, Meeka, or Isabella. Meeka thought that was harsh, but she didn't argue with him. He was a grown man, and he could make his own decisions.

Meeka was still on bed rest, but eventually, she would be running the streets. She had enough things circulating in her head so the less stress, the better. Her phone began to ring, and she rushed to answer the call. Forty was now in Pensacola, Florida visiting family and Meeka was excited to hear from him.

"Big Forty, what up?" Meeka laughed.

"Meek Milly, what's up girl?" He asked and laughed.

"Nothing much, just cooling outside, you know me. I'm trying to enjoy some of this downtime before I go head first in the game."

"I feel you on that, but what about the promise you kept?"

"What Hustle doesn't know won't hurt him. I have things to do. Hustle needs to chill out and be cool."

"I hear you, but let me know what he says when you tell him that." He laughed.

"Like I said before, what he doesn't know won't hurt him." Meeka laughed.

"I guess Meeka, but besides that, what's going on?"

"Nothing much, just trying to figure everything out. Hustle is serious about this move Forty. He found a house in San Diego!"

"Are you serious?" Forty asked.

"Yes and I am, but I wish I wasn't. I don't know what to say or do anymore. I'm ready to shut down and give up on everything, but I know I can't."

"You're right, you know you can't. Moving isn't a bad thing Meeka. I'm not sure why you have that in your head. You have to get out of that polluted town and see better. Meeka you need to do better for the sake of Isabella."

"You are sound exactly like Brink right now. I'm not ready to leave behind all this money. Just with the strip club money, I can retire. Am I really supposed to give this up for love?" Meeka asked.

"You know my answer, but you need to ask yourself that. You need to decide soon, or it's going to be too late. Hustle loves you, and you won't find anyone else like him. He puts up with a lot of your shit Meek, be honest." Forty said.

"That's by choice Forty. He doesn't HAVE to do anything his heart doesn't desire." Meeka snapped.

"It's easy to say that when you're not in his shoes. The only thing I ask is that you sit down and think about it. Don't lose something good for temporary things. If Hustle leaves your ass today or tomorrow, none of that money will hold you at night. Trust me, I didn't want to leave Opelousas either, but I knew it was time. If I wouldn't have, I would have killed someone, and I wouldn't have cared about the aftermath. Austin is playing too many games and tampering with everyone's freedom."

"The way you left was foul Forty, and you know it," Meeka mumbled and rolled her eyes. Forty exhaled and dropped his head. He gently rubbed the back of his head and exhaled again.

"I'm sorry I left the way did, but I felt like that was the best way to do it. It's too many bad and good memories there that I was holding onto. I rather leave on my own instead of in a box or being escorted by the FED's." He said.

"I understand Forty, and I can't lie, I was pissed when you left. I was being selfish about the situation, and I'm sorry. You had the right to leave because that's what YOU wanted to do, but it's not what I wanted you to do. You're young and have your entire life ahead of you. You need to travel the world, fall in love again, and have a dozen of babies."

"A dozen Meeka, that's a lot?" Forty laughed.

"Well maybe two or three, but you know what I mean. You deserve to be happy Gavin. I know Camille would want you to be happy. Shit, she probably sent someone to you, but you don't know it. You know it is okay to love and be in love again. You're a good man, make another woman happy."

"I know, but I'm not sure if I'm ready. I guess when the timing is right I'll know."

"I guess so, but open your heart up and let a little love into it," Meeka said.

"What about you Meeka?"

"What about me?" Meeka asked.

"Since you have all the answers for me, what about yourself? I'm telling you now don't let Hustle slip out of your hands. Just imagine how the women will be at his feet if you two break up."

"It sounds like someone has a crush on Brink." Meeka laughed.

"Very funny Meek, but I'm serious. What are you going to do? We all know time doesn't wait for anyone, and you are no exception."

"I'm old in this game baby and being in this little town is the best thing for me." Meeka chuckled.

"Shut up Meek, you're talking as if you are sixty-five years old." Forty burst into laughter, and so did Meeka. Meeka was only in her thirties, but she felt like she was in her sixties.

"Lil' brother that's what I feel like. Enough of that though, how is Pensacola?" Meeka asked.

"It's nice as hell. You should see the beach houses. I swear Meek, your name is written all over them."

"Oh really, is that your way of getting me to visit or move?" Meeka asked and laughed.

"A little bit of both. I know you would love it here. The sand is soft and perfect. The water is crystal blue, the atmosphere is clear, and the sky is even clearer. I'm not sure if I'm in heaven or paradise." He laughed.

"I'll talk to Hustle about visiting soon. Maybe we might run into Pedro at the airport, the gas station, or somewhere, shit I don't know," Meeka rolled her eyes and ran her fingers through her loose hair. Thinking about Pedro's disappearance always put her in an awkward place.

"I'm guessing you guys haven't heard from him yet?"

"No, and honestly Forty, I don't think he's going to contact us. Deep down inside, I think it's more to why he left without saying anything to anyone."

"Do you think he knows about that thing?" Forty asked.

"I think he does and that could be the prime reason he left. Brink and I have put Pedro in some fucked up situations, and he never folded under pressure. For the last time, we put him in a situation, and he probably has folded."

"Damn, that makes a lot of sense. I'm glad he didn't pull a sucker move." Forty said.

"I know, but I wish I had the chance to tell him why. Then he would fully understand why I did it. A part of me didn't want to do it, but I had to. It was business and personal. You know I hate mixing the two together."

"Fuck it, it's done. You can't take it back. Has Hustle said anything about Dro?" Forty asked.

"Not really, but sometimes I try to talk to him about him."

"What does he say?"

"He doesn't say much. Majority of the time he brushes it off. I guess that's his way of dealing with it and I won't ever understand that."

"Shit happens, I never liked him anyway."

Meeka spotted a 2014 pickup truck approaching her house, and she knew it was Marlo. She slowly stood to her feet and tightened the belt on her robe. The closer the truck drove, Marlo smiled at his sister. For some reason, he was happy to see her. Meeka hadn't seen Marlo in two weeks so she happy to see him as well.

"That was harsh, but I have to go. Marlo just got here."

"Okay, tell that nigga hit me up when he leaves." Forty said.

"Bet." Meeka disconnected the call and dropped her phone into her pocket. Marlo grabbed his yellow hard hat and duffle bag then he jumped out of the truck. He shook the driver's hand, and the driver drove off. This was Marlo's first time working and seeing him in dirty work clothes made Meeka proud. Dust and dirt covered his long sleeve cream colored thermal and ripped jeans. His eyes were low and heavy which meant he was sleepy. That made Meeka more proud of him because that meant he was working hard.

"Look at you little brother. For a moment, you made me want to get a job." Meeka stood to her feet and smiled at Marlo. She stood at the edge of the steps and embraced him with a hug. She didn't care that dust covered the front of her robe. Meeka simply brushed the dust off her robe and sat down.

"For a quick moment huh, that damn Meek."

"It was a very quick moment. You know I'm not with that nine to five shit." Meeka laughed.

"We all can't be *Money Making Meeka*."

"We all can't be Marlo either. What's good baby?" Meeka asked.

"Nothing, just glad to be back at home. They were killing us in Pittsburg. My damn back is killing me," Marlo rubbed his lower back and yawned.

Meeka smacked her lips and said, "Damn bro, this your first job, and you're complaining already?" She joked.

"Hell no I'm not complaining, but you know us hood niggas." He laughed.

"Right, but I'm proud of you. I was on the phone with Forty, and he said to call him."

"Oh yea, what was he talking about?" Marlo asked.

"Same ole shit, but he asked about Pedro," Meeka said.

"Is there something new with that?"

"I wish there was, but no. I guess we'll never see Pedro again. Maybe it's a good thing. He knew a lot and suspected a lot as well," Meeka shrugged her shoulders and turned away. She didn't want to get too deep into the conversation, but she was sure Marlo had a few things he wanted to say.

right about that, but Pedro is a solid dude."

"He's solid for how though? Something in my heart tells me Pedro left for more than one reason."

"Are you serious?" Marlo asked.

"Yes, I'm very serious. I think Pedro didn't want to lie or he knew I had something to do with Juju. I swear

Marlo, I can feel it, and I know my gut feeling isn't steering me wrong."

"I don't know Meek, you could be right, but we'll never know the truth."

"Don't you find it strange how he just up and…left. He kind of like disappeared in thin air. He didn't tell anyone or contact anyone once he made it to his destination. It kind of sounds like a bizarre movie to me, but I could be pulling information out of my ass."

"It is 'strange' how he left, but Forty did the same thing." He said.

"That's true, but Forty also contacted everyone once he made it to Florida. With Camille's death and being tied into this shit with me, Forty had every right to leave."

"I guess, but we can't dwell on Pedro. I know I'm sure not dwelling on him. I hope he has a suit of armor on and God is watching over him." Marlo laughed and tossed his hands in the air. Meeka didn't want to laugh, but she couldn't control it. Marlo was right, they couldn't dwell on Pedro. It was clear that Pedro wasn't doing the same and didn't want to be bothered by anyone from home. That included the ones he once called friends.

"I swear I hate you. A suit of armor Marlo, really?"

"Yea really, if he calls or comes back that's cool. If he doesn't, oh well. I won't lose any sleep over Pedro…whatever his last name is."

"You're right. I have enough on my plate to worry about. When are you leaving again? I want to take you to dinner or something. I'm so proud of you right now." Meeka tapped Marlo on the arm and smiled.

Marlo held Meeka's hand tightly and replied, "Next week we're going to Florida to work for three weeks. I'm excited about this welding job." Not many people knew it, but Marlo graduated from a technical college with a welding trade certificate. He didn't put the trade to use until now. Marlo only enrolled in college because his former girlfriend pushed him to do it. Meeka wasn't sure why he decided to get a job now, but she didn't question it.

"Make that money little brother, that's all we know."

"Hell yea, if you don't work, you don't eat."

"Are you going to still hustle?" Meeka asked.

"I think I'm done with it, Meek. The city and our names are too hot right now. I'm not trying to see the inside of a jail."

"I'm not trying to see the inside of a jail either, but its new money to be made. You know I have a thing for new money," Meeka rubbed her hands and grinned.

"I thought you were on bed rest?" Marlo asked.

"I am, but once I'm cleared you know it is back to the money."

"Listen to your body Meek and take your time. The way these clowns trap around here, the money will still be there." He joked.

"You're right. I don't have much to worry about." Meeka laughed and shook her head.

"I'm sorry I didn't make it to the hospital to see you. I can't lie, you had me worried sick about you." Marlo said.

"Marlo, you don't have to be sorry. I told you to stay where you were. I'm a big girl, and I can handle myself." She laughed.

"I know you are sis, but what the hell happened?" Meeka sighed, and Marlo sat closer to her. She softly grabbed his sister's hand and waited for her to respond.

Meeka wasn't sure where to start, but she said, "Honestly Marlo, I don't know. One minute Sydney and I were talking then about thirty minutes later I was in bed sweating like a Muslim in a pig factory. My chest was pounding, but it also felt like bricks were sitting on my chest. I didn't want to wake Hustle, but I was scared out of my mind. We talked about what was wrong, and I slowly calmed down. Once I got in the shower, things started to change, for the worse."

"What do you mean?" Marlo asked.

"I started hearing Juju's voice in my head, and I started seeing blood."

"What?"

"Yes, and the blood was everywhere. I couldn't get it off me. It's like her blood was coming out of the shower head and my entire body was covered in it. Brink took me to the emergency room, and the doctor said I was suffering from anxiety. He monitored me for three days, gave me a prescription, and sent me on my way. Just when I thought that was enough drama, I was wrong."

"What else happened?" Marlo patted his deep back pockets searching for his pack of cigarettes. Once he retrieved them, he slid his hand into his front pocket and pulled out a red lighter. He slowly lit a cigarette and took a hit. He tried to hand it to Meeka, but she pushed it away and said, "I quit, but thanks," Marlo nodded his head and shrugged his shoulders.

"Tori's ass came here to 'help' Hustle with Isabella and I. You know that went in every direction, but right."

"Damn, another argument with her? I'm surprised you haven't put that iron in her life yet." Marlo laughed.

"Hmmm, don't think I haven't thought about it a few times. If I didn't love her son, POW, POW, POW!" Meeka pretended to hold a gun and released imaginary bullets in the air. Marlo flicked the remainder of the cigarette in the grass and laughed.

"I'm talking about jumping on her car and acting like Marlo Mike."

"Hell yea, but as soon as she stepped foot in my house, she started taking shots at me. Hustle left for five minutes, and we got into an argument. I tossed her ass out, and I didn't care how Brink felt about the situation. One thing leads to another, and the truth finally came out."

"What's that?" Marlo asked.

"She doesn't like me because I'm light skin and I have long hair."

"HUH, did I hear that correctly?"

"Yes, you sure did. She said I reminded her of all the women her husband cheated on her with. Every single woman was light skin and had long hair, but that doesn't give her the right to take it out on me." Meeka said.

"That shit is crazy yo. Hustle's mom is old, but that bitch is bad as fuck." Marlo laughed.

"Right, but I guess she doesn't see that. Then again, how could she see it? How would you feel if you were in her shoes? I probably would hate me as well. Hustle even got her to admit that she didn't always like Isabella."

"What, are you serious Meek?"

"I wish I wasn't Marlo, but I'm dead ass serious. This entire time I thought she hated me because I was 'stealing' Brink from her. I was sssoooo wrong, and for a period of time, my child had to suffer for it." Meeka's eyes began to fill with tears, and her lips started to tremble. Marlo's smile faded away and his shoulders slowly dropped. He hated seeing his sister cry, so he gave her a hug. Meeka wiped her wet face on her shirt and deeply sighed.

"Hey, this is not your fault."

"Are you sure it isn't because it seems like it is. Everyone has a problem, and somehow it all comes down on me." Meeka whimpered.

"Meeka none of this is your fault, stop beating yourself up. If you could, I know you would control everything around you. You can't, and you have to accept it for what it is. Tori's a pretty but crazy ass bitch. With all that money Hustle has, he needs to get his mom some professional help." Marlo laughed.

"One part of me feels sorry for her, but the other part of me doesn't. She is now a complete joke to me, and I don't want Isabella at her house anymore. I'm fine with her visiting her, but she will not be left alone with Tori."

"Do you think she's ever harmed her?" Marlo asked.

"I'm not sure Marlo, but I hope she hasn't. Brink asked her that question, but we couldn't get an answer."

"Why not?"

"Brink was so upset with his mom, he wanted to hit her. Before he even attempted to raise his hand, she ran out of the room and left."

"Wow, not Hustle huh? He's always so calm and cool, I can't see him getting upset to the point he would hit a woman."

"I know, and that's something I never want to witness. I have a question, and I want you to be completely honest with me,"

"What's up sis, what's wrong?" Marlo asked.

"Do you ever think about how our lives would have been if our parents weren't killed?" Meeka asked.

"Yea, I think about it, but I try my best to leave it out of my thoughts," Marlo said.

"Why?" Meeka asked.

"When I do think about it, it puts me deep in my feelings. Sometimes it puts me in a dark place, and I shut down. I don't want to be bothered with anyone and get full of pills. I pop a tab and forget what put me in my feelings."

Marlo laughed, but that was only to disguise his true feelings. Meeka could see the chill bumps forming on his arms, and she was surprised. It was obvious that it was truth to what he was saying and Meeka was hoping he would tell her everything without her asking him.

"Why is this my first time hearing this Marlo?"

"Because I don't like talking about it. I always wondered if one of us was home that night if things would have turned out differently. I know you would have put that iron on them Meek, no question about it." Marlo laughed.

"Sometimes I ask God why our lives had to be so hard. We are the prime examples of getting it out the mud. I don't know many people who can hustle hard like you, me, and Santana," Meeka stood to her feet and slowly paced back and forth on the porch. Her porch was wide and long, so she had plenty of room. With the emotions that were running through her body, she was tempted to drop to her knees and begin to cry.

"We have been through a lot, but we pulled through it. We don't have to do a lot of the things we did to survive. Do you remember when we broke into that house and stole that food?" He asked and laughed.

"Hell yea, how could I forget about that? That was the best ham sandwich and chips I ever had. Our parents were eating T-bone steaks while your feet were on my shoulders climbing into a window. While you were sleeping, I cried that night like a baby. I promised myself I would never be that kind of parent.

"I cried myself to sleep that night too. That entire night didn't make any sense to me."

"Why did they treat us like shit Marlo? We were harmless kids, and we didn't deserve that."

"I know we didn't Meek, but fuck the past," Marlo said.

Meeka could feel word vomit coming, but she was afraid of the aftermath.

"Ma- Ma- Marlo, I did it." Meeka's shuttering made it hard for Marlo to hear her. He pulled his chair closer to her and asked, "What did you do?"

"I- I – I – I killed our parents, and I'm not sorry about it. I will never be sorry because not one bone in my body has sympathy for what I did. My dad purposely killed my mom just so he could be with your mom. Then they tricked me out to different men and women. That's why I hated when you would leave to visit your dad. I was alone with them, and they would make me do some many disgusting things. Your mom, she's the person who introduced me to escorting."

"Don't feel bad Meeka. They did it to me as well. I'm glad you killed them before I did." Meeka's neck became stiff, and her eyes stretched wide. The words that rolled off of Marlo's tongue wasn't something she expected to hear. They locked eyes with each other, and neither said anything. The sad looks on their faces and their tears said it all. Marlo and Meeka no longer had to hide their terrible childhood from one another.

Chapter 3

Tonight was Sunday which was date night for Sydney and Jason. Sydney was enjoying every minute of spending time with him. Since they both were budgeting on a teacher's salary, a small restaurant was perfect. Mello Mushroom was located in Lafayette, Louisiana and it was Sydney's favorite restaurant for various reasons. Mainly because it was, she and Xavier's first date and they often visited the place. Sydney constantly looked over her shoulder hoping she wouldn't see Xavier standing behind her or walking into the restaurant.

Even though she insisted on having dinner there, it still put her in an awkward place. It slightly made her walk down memory lane, and she had Xavier on her mind. She tried not to think about him, but she couldn't help it. Xavier tried everything in his power to win Sydney's heart back, but it seemed like nothing worked. He didn't care though. He wasn't ready to give up on the woman he truly loved.

"Are you sure you want to eat here? It's a seafood place up the road, and the food is to die for," Jason closed the menu and reached into his pocket and grabbed five ones and dropped them on the table. He stood to his feet, but Sydney grabbed his arm and laughed.

"I'm sure I want to eat here. The pizza is great. Now sit down and be cool," Jason shrugged his shoulders and sat down. Sydney handed him the menu and reopened it. She slightly smiled and laughed to herself. Sydney didn't need him to take her to an expensive place to have a good time. As long as she was spending time with him, it didn't matter where they were.

"I think I'm going to get the shrimp special pizza. Yea, that's what I'm going to get." Sydney said.

"What comes on it?" Jason asked.

"It has boiled gulf shrimp, spinach, artichoke, mozzarella cheese, and Roma tomatoes."

"Ugh, yuck! I'll get a steak and cheese calzone." Jason said.

"That sounds good," Sydney closed her menu and reached for her glass of water. She took a few sips then she moved the glass to the side.

"How is your friend Meeka been since she left the hospital?" Jason asked.

"She's good. When I left her house, she was in bed. Her brother got back in town Friday, so he's there as well." Sydney didn't tell Jason the truth about why Meeka was admitted to the hospital. The only thing he needed to know was that she wasn't feeling well.

"Her brother, I didn't know she had a brother?" Jason asked.

"Yea, you can call him her stepbrother. His name is Marlo, and he is just as crazy as her. Their parents dated and they have been close ever since. When their parents died, it made them closer than ever."

"Damn, when did their parents die?"

"I think it was the night of Meeka's eighteenth birthday. Someone broke into the house and killed them, but luckily Meeka nor Marlo wasn't home."

"Woowww, did they ever find out who did it?" Jason asked.

"No, the case went cold quick," Sydney said.

"That is crazy man. Where are your other friends?"

"Who?" Sydney asked.

"Correct me if I'm wrong, but I'm talking about Jupiter and Spencer. Did they go back to Kansas or wherever they came from?" Sydney wanted to laugh, but she cracked a smile instead. She always laughed when Jason mention Spencer and Jupiter because he believed that was their names and true identities.

"Uummm yea, they left three days ago."

"Oh okay, but anyway, how was your day?" Jason asked.

"My day was good, I can't complain at all. Church was also good, I needed to be there. I was sitting on the first row with the first lady. It felt good to be back in the Lord's house, for a moment my faith slipped away."

"I'm glad you gathered yourself together. Why did you stop going to church?" Jason asked.

Before replying, Sydney took another sip of her drink. She cleared her throat a little, then said, "With everything that's going on in my life with my husband and friends, I wanted to hide from the world," Sydney tried to finish her sentence, but she noticed an angry pregnant woman staring in their direction. A woman sat across the table talking to her, but she completely ignored her and kept her eyes on the back of Jason's head. She was staring hard and hate-filled her eyes. Sydney was surprised that Jason couldn't feel the hate burning the back of his head.

"Hi, are yall ready to order now?" The waitress stood next to Sydney with her pen and notebook in her hand while smacking on some gum. Her pale white skin color and long royal blue hair made her look like a punk rock chick. Her nose, lips, and chin was pierced, but her look didn't fit her voice. It was soft and sweet. She was a perfect example of not judging a book by its cover.

"Yea Kristen, we're ready. I'll take a small shrimp special pizza. He'll take a steak and cheese calzone and heavy on the cheese," Kristen quickly jotted the order down then she slipped her pin into her pocket. She smiled at Sydney and said, "Okay, let me take those menus, and I'll put those orders in right way," Jason and Sydney handed Kristen the menus, and she walked away.

"I was kind of embarrassed to face the public. My husband's bashing my name and character as if we never loved one another. I gave that man the best of me, and all I asked for was a smooth divorce." Sydney continued.

"I can only imagine what you're going through Syd, honestly. The only advice I can give you is to stay strong and keep your head up. Before you know it, the bullshit will pass by like a wave. It can't rain forever the sun will eventually come out."

"That's the question, when will the sun come out? It seems like it is getting overshadowed by these dark clouds. Every time it seems like things are getting better, life throws another curve ball at me. I'm to the point I want to give up and throw the towel in."

"You can't give up baby girl. You have too much to give up. In your son's eyes, I bet you're the strongest woman they know."

"You're talking like your young ass been through some real problems." Sydney laughed.

"No, I haven't gone through a divorce, but I witnessed my aunt go through one. My uncle Rich showed his ass like a donkey." He shook his head.

"Was he that bad?" Sydney asked.

"Hell yea, my uncle showed a side of himself we never knew existed. He was so bitter about my auntie leaving him, he tried to kill her."

"What, are you serious?"

"I'm very serious, he ran her off the road. She and her daughter were on their way home. She crashed into a tree, but by the grace of God, they didn't die. Thank God she was wearing her seatbelt, and Audrika was strapped properly in her car seat. The doctors said if they wouldn't have had their seatbelts on, they would have been ejected from the car."

"Wow, I'm kind of afraid now. Your uncle sounds a lot like my husband." Sydney said.

"Don't be scared. Always be aware, especially when he's in your presence."

"I will, I don't trust Austin one bit anymore. How is your auntie by the way?" Sydney asked.

"Aunt Lacey is doing well. She remarried and had two more kids. I guess she got her happy ending like she always wanted."

"That's good for her. I guess there is happiness after a divorce. I hope I get my happiness, I think I deserve it." Sydney said.

"You will Sydney, it takes time. You know nothing happens overnight." Jason said.

"That is true, but what about your uncle? How is he doing nowadays?"

"That clown is in Lafayette Parish Jail serving time for violating his parole. I think he has a girlfriend, but he's probably using her. You never know with him, and I really don't care. As long as it's not you in jail, I'm good," Jason grabbed Sydney's hand and smiled. She smiled as well, and her eyes began to scan the building. The woman was still looking at her, and now she was making Sydney uncomfortable.

"It's crazy how your aunt and uncle remind me of Austin and myself."

"You know she would be the perfect person to vent to and get advice from. My aunt is a good woman, and she wouldn't steer you wrong." Jason said.

"Thanks, Jason, I would like that. I need motivation to push me through this. I'm sorry, I'm trying to give you my undivided attention, but I can't." Sydney said.

"Why not, what's wrong?" He asked and laughed.

"Don't look yet, but there is this woman that is staring at us. She's been staring at us for a while now." The woman seems to be about six months pregnant but looks ready to deliver at any moment. Her hair is blonde, but her roots were black. She needs a serious coloring done to her hair. Her skin tone was brown like cinnamon, and her face was covered with pregnancy acne. Besides the heavy acne, she was beautiful and reminded Sydney of an African queen.

She paid more attention to Sydney that she didn't realize the waiter was waiting for her to take the checkbook out of her hand.

Sydney sarcastically pointed at the checkbook and giggled. The woman shook her head as if she was confused and turned to the waiter. While she handed the waiter her credit card, she rolled her eyes at Sydney. Sydney was confused, but she didn't mind entertaining the strange woman.

"What woman?" Jason asked.

"The woman behind us, you can look now," Jason turned around and glanced at the woman, then turned back around.

"Oh, her," Jason said.

"I'm guessing you know her since you said that," Sydney replied.

"I've seen her around town before, that's all. I think her name is Mariah something with an M." He said.

"Oh, okay, maybe she's starring hard because she likes you. You know you are a very handsome guy." Sydney grabbed Jason's hand and long stroked it. She only wanted to make the girl jealous. By the evil stares she was giving Sydney, the mission was accomplished.

"Maybe she likes you, she looks like a dyke." Jason joked.

"She does not look like a dyke Jason. That girl is beautiful, and she's probably in a relationship with her child's father. If she is a dyke, why is she pregnant?" Sydney asked and whispered.

"Shit, I don't know why. You act like you have never seen a pregnant dyke before. Half of them aren't gay they do it because it's a trend."

"That's true, but I don't think she's a dyke," Sydney replied.

"I guess, but enough about her. I was thinking about something." Jason said.

"What were you thinking about?"

"There is this Boosie concert in Shreveport next month, do you want to go?" He asked.

"A Boosie concert, damn, I haven't attended a Boosie concert in years." She said.

"That's because he was locked up for a while, duh." He laughed.

"Oh yea, that's true, and I was stupid for saying that." She snickered and covered her face. Jason removed her hands from her face and said, "Don't feel stupid just don't say that to anyone else." He chuckled.

"Trust me I won't."

"I'm taking that as a yes. I think we both can use a little vacation. We can stay for the weekend. Shreveport has a nice boardwalk I want to take you to. You can ask your friend Tameeka to babysit the boys. I'm sure she wouldn't mind, they are always there anyway."

"Hmmm, I do need a little time away from home. When exactly is this concert, I want to ask her when I get back home?"

"Okay, and it's the tenth. She better say yea, I'm itching to spend some real time with you." He smiled.

"Me too, I haven't seen an adult scenery in months. Have you ever been so tired of a place that it makes your stomach turn?" Sydney grabbed her stomach and pretended to be in pain.

"Yes, I know the feeling. That's how I felt about Abbeville. That town is too small for the amount of crime that does down. Three years ago, I lost a childhood friend because of violence. His name was Jackson, a real laid back guy. He was loved by many people but also hated by a lot as well. When he was killed, it felt like the city died as well."

"Aawwww, how did he die?" Sydney asked.

"He was killed on the basketball court, and his six-year-old daughter was with him. Those ruthless niggas didn't care about her presence. A witness said she heard twenty shots before she ran and she was still hearing shots. His daughter was hit twice, once in the arm and once in the leg. That poor child is going to be scared for life. She watched her dad die in front of her, and it's nothing she could do about it."

"Oh my God, that is scary, my heart is breaking. That poor little girl didn't deserve to be a part of that. People can be heartless and for the wrong reasons!"

"When a nigga has beef with you, they won't stop until they get you. They'll come for you and everyone you hold close to your heart." Jason said.

"He also sounds like my husband. Since I filed for divorce, he's taken his anger out on everything, especially my friends. It's crazy how he feels that Tameeka is the reason I wanted to divorce him. In my heart, I still think he pulled the trigger on Santana. I could be wrong, or maybe that's what I want to believe." Sydney turned away, but Jason grabbed her hand and gave it a kiss. Jason could tell she was sad, but he had to change that quick.

"Hey, no tears tonight beautiful, okay?"

"Okay," Sydney smiled then she leaned forward and gave Jason a kiss. She was shocked at how much public display of affection she exposed to him in the restaurant. She was never the type to do any of this, but she couldn't help the way Jason made her feel.

A few seconds later, Kristen approached the table with a black and oval tray sitting on her shoulder. Steamy plates sat on the tray, and it made Sydney's stomach growl loudly. She was embarrassed and hoped that Jason couldn't hear her stomach.

"Finally, I was starving and ready to go in the kitchen myself." He laughed. Kristen giggled a little and placed the plates in front of Sydney and Jason. Then she grabbed their empty and half-empty glasses from the table.

"Do you guys need anything else?"

"Just a refill on those drinks," Jason pointed at the glasses with his fork and took a bit of his calzone. He looked at Sydney's pizza and pretended to gag. She flared her nose at him and smiled.

"You don't know what you're missing Jason, tell him, Kristen." Sydney grinned.

"She's right about that. The shrimp special is one of our popular dishes."

"What's the most popular?" Jason asked. Kristen hesitated to answer, but she closed her eyes and said, "The Calzone." Sydney gasped and rolled her eyes. Jason shook his head and pointed at his plate. He laughed then he took another bite.

"I'll be right back with your drinks." She said.

"Do you ever think about transferring?" Sydney asked.

"Transferring what?" Jason asked with a mouth full of food.

"Do you ever think about transferring to another school?"

"Oh that, sometimes I do. I never go through with it clearly. Those kids are getting worse by the second, and I pray to God I don't knock one of their little asses out."

"We are saying the same prayer because it's this one little girl in my class I can't wait until she makes eighteen, I'm going to beat her lil' ass to the ground."

As Jason and Sydney laughed, the woman that sat across from them held on the corner of the table and climbed to her feet. She slowly walked past their table and glanced over her shoulder. Jason ignored her, but Sydney stared at her until she walked out of the restaurant. Sydney waited for the woman to turn around, but she didn't. Sydney laughed and sipped on her drink.

Two hours later, Sydney and Jason were ending their night. They walked out of the restaurant holding hands while conversing and laughing. Sydney couldn't get enough of Jason, and she didn't want the date or night to end. As Jason reached to open the door, he noticed something was wrong from a distant.

"Damn it, my tire is busted. I must have rolled over a nail or something," Jason smacked his lips and slapped his hands on his front pockets. Then he reached into his pocket and grabbed his cell phone. As he dialed roadside assistance, he walked to his truck. When he noticed the other three tires were also flat, he dropped his phone, and his body froze. The sound of the phone falling grabbed Sydney's attention. She ran to his side and asked, "What's wrong?" Once she noticed what he was pointing at, she gasped and said, "What the hell, I don't think you rolled over that many nails."

"What the hell is really going on!" He shouted and kicked his car, but quickly pulled back. He hopped in a circle and held his foot. It was in major pain, and Sydney laughed. She couldn't believe how stupid and immature he was for kicking his car. It wasn't the car's fault that he 'rolled' over several nails.

"I don't know, but are you sure you don't have any crazy ex-girlfriends in the neighborhood?" Sydney laughed, but her question was serious. She found it impossible that

Jason rolled over four nails, but as of now that was the only conclusion.

"I don't think so." He laughed and squatted to the ground to retrieve his phone. Sydney gave him a stale look and softly kicked him on his leg. He laughed louder and held her leg to control his balance. Then he wiped his dusty phone on his pants' pocket and extended his body straight.

"Don't play with me, Jason. I don't have time to fight anyone tonight."

"That's the last thing you should worry about sweetheart," Jason kissed Sydney on the lips, and within seconds she started to blush. Her cheeks turned warm and rosy red and her heart started to beat rapidly. Jason had her feeling like she was a high school senior asking the captain of the football team to prom. He took a step back and began to laugh. He couldn't take his eyes off her red cheeks. He brushed the back side of his hands against them, and his smile grew wider and larger.

"What's going on with your cheeks, they're red hot? Kind of like your red ass, but then again, nothing is hot as you." Jason kissed her again making her blush even more. She covered her face and laughed. She didn't want Jason to see how much he could make her smile with his weak and cheesy pickup lines.

"I don't know Jason, I think this youngin' is driving me crazy. I still find it hard to believe you don't have a girlfriend. I think eventually she's going to come out of the bushes and appear at school." Sydney laughed.

"I tend to drive the ladies crazy every now and then," Jason grabbed a hand full of Sydney's ass and buried his bald nails deep into her ass cheeks. Sydney's body pushed closer to him, and she wrapped her arms around his neck. She passionately kissed Jason, but she knew it wouldn't go further than kissing. Surprisingly they only had sex three times and none of those times were at his home. Sydney thought it was a little weird that he never invited her to his place, but she always brushed it off. Without clarifying it with him, she assumed he had a stay at home girlfriend that no one knew anything about.

"Every now and then huh," With her arms still wrapped around Jason's neck, she modestly backed away. She sized him up and down, and he nibbled on her cheeks and laughed.

"I'm glad I can make you laugh on this wonderful night."

"This night was wonderful until this shit happened," Jason used his phone to point at the tires and shook his head. Every time he stared at his flat tires, he began to get angry again. He started to dial numbers, and quickly whispered, "I'm going to call for help."

"Okay." She whispered back, and he walked away.

Sydney leaned against the car while Jason talked to the roadside assistant operator. Her voice was squeaky and upbeat, and Sydney hated it. She was glad she wasn't the person who had to make the phone call. Once she thought of phone calls, she gasped and rushed to pull her phone out of her bra. She dialed Meeka's number and waited for her to answer. By the third ring, Meeka answered the phone yawning and clearing her throat.

"Meek,"

"What's up Syd, is something wrong?" Meeka asked.

"Yea, kind of," Sydney replied.

"What's wrong and do you need me?"

"No, I don't need you. Jason and I walked out of the restaurant, and we noticed his tires were flat. I'm going to get home later than I expected, is that cool?"

"Girl you're good, the boys bathed, ate, and is now in bed. Are all the tires on a flat?" Meeka asked.

"Girl yes, all fucking four tires, can you believe that shit?! I guess he rolled over some nails or something." Sydney said.

"If all four tires are flat it sounds like someone put the nails or a nice screwdriver in his tires. If you can, check to see what area of the tire is busted."

"Okay, hold on," Sydney spoke in a whisper and stretched her neck to get a better view of Jason. He was pacing in front of his car while he gave the operator directions. He didn't notice that Sydney was on the phone, so she squatted to the ground. It was dark, but the parking lot had enough lighting for her to see. She ran her hand on the tire and felt a slash on the sidewalls of the tire. The tire slash was at least twenty-four inches long and deep. Sydney looked to her right to make sure Jason was still on the phone, and he was. She hopped to the left back tire and did the same thing. It was also slashed, but the slash was longer. Sydney was now confused and wanted to check the front tires as well. Jason was standing too close to his car, and she knew she would get caught. Instead, she stood to her feet and wiped her oily hand on her jeans.

"Meek, are you still there?" Sydney asked.

"Yea Syd, what did you find?" Meeka asked.

"Well both back tires were cut, and it looks like it was cut with a butcher knife. If not a butcher knife it was something big."

"Really?" Meeka asked.

"Yes, and it was the sidewalls were the slash was," Sydney said.

"That's crazy did you check the front tires?" Meeka asked.

"No, he's standing in front of his car talking to roadside assistance. It's not adding up, but I won't say anything. We had a good night, and I plan to keep it that way." Sydney said.

"Let me guess, is Stella getting her groove back tonight?" Meeka asked and laughed.

"Hell no, we don't have sex like that. I told you that, but clearly you don't believe me," Sydney covered her mouth and chuckled. The wind began to blow lightly, and her hair was dancing with the wind.

"That's because I thought you were lying and being secretive. Oh yea, Xavier stopped by about an hour ago. I wanted to text you, but I didn't want to bother you." Meeka said.

"Oh, he did. What did he want?" Now that the conversation shifted to Xavier, Sydney's tone suddenly changed. It was flat and low, and she wasn't concerned about why he stopped by.

"He wanted to drop off his favorite girl a few things. He asked where you were and of course, I lied. I told him you were at Walmart getting supplies for your students. Please text or call him, just say you're in bed and you'll call tomorrow." Meeka demanded.

"Thanks for lying, but he shouldn't be in my business." Sydney snapped and rolled her neck as if Meeka could see her body language.

"Anyways crazy lady, I see your favorite candy, chips, and beverages in a nice basket. Attached to it is a simple, but cute card. I'll read to you what it says. 'No special occasion, just something sweet for my sweet girl. Enjoy baby, and I love you. XOXO Xavier.' Aaawwww Syd that is so cute and thoughtful of him," Meeka silently read the letter to herself again and smiled. She pressed it against her heart then she placed it ontop of the basket.

"Nothing is sweet about him trying to get me fat. If I gain all that weight that will be another reason for him to cheat on me. Nope Meek, I'm not having that shit again!"

"We call that relationship weight baby and nothing is wrong with that. When Brink and I first got together, I gained ten pounds. That was the best ten pounds of my life." Meeka laughed and grabbed a chocolate bar out of the basket. Then she flopped on her couch and ripped the tip of the paper off the chocolate. She shoved a piece into her mouth and rubbed her eyes. She was also getting sleepy and wanted to get in bed.

"Call it what you want, but that doesn't change anything. He still cheated on me, and I'm still not sure if I can get over it and move forward." Sydney said.

"Okay Syd, I understand that, but the guy is trying hard to win you back," Meeka said.

"Before you were ready to knock his head off his shoulders for cheating on me, and you were glad I met Jason, but now you're feeling bad for Xavier. How did you switch sides like that Meek?"

"Look, it's not about switching sides, it's about forgiveness. I'm putting myself in his shoes, and I understand how he feels. When I slept with Stevie behind Hustle's back, I thought he was done with me for good. Boy, did I have some sleepless nights because of my wondering mind."

"So, what are you saying I should do? Are you saying I should leave Jason alone and run back to Xavier like everything is okay? Jason hasn't done me any wrong, and I don't think I should leave him so suddenly. He's young, but he's a really good guy!"

"Hey, I don't have a problem with the Jason cat. I can't pass any judgment on him because I only met him once. On the other hand, I do know Xavier, and I can tell he's sincere and sorry. Let's be honest for a minute homegirl, Jason is young and temporary, but Xavier is stable and forever. That is someone you can build a future with. That WAS someone you were building a future with. I know you love him and deep down inside you don't want throw that love away. Another thing, let's not forget how we were wilding when we were Jason's age. I bet I had my mom and dad rolling in their graves. Rest in Peace mom, but fuck you dad." Meeka laughed and waved her middle finger to the ceiling. She was sure her dad was looking down at her and shaking his head. Her mom, on the other hand, was probably asking God to remove the hate from her daughter's heart.

The weather was perfect, and the wind was blowing smoothly. Sydney could feel the chill bumps forming on her back and arms, but she didn't mind it. She loved the way the wind was dancing against her smooth skin. Her eyes began to wonder, and she spotted a car sitting in the parking lot with the lights off. The car seemed out of place because the passenger and driver were sitting low and staring in Sydney's direction.

"I have to go Meek I'll call you when we're on our back to Opelousas." Sydney disconnected the call and placed her phone on top of the trunk. She tried to squint her eyes to get a better view of the women, but they covered their faces.

"What the fuck?" She mumbled.

As the driver ducked to stay hidden from Sydney and started the car, Sydney's attention turned to the passenger. She tried her best to hide from Sydney too, but her large forehead was fully exposed. From a distance, it looked a lot like the pregnant woman that was in the restaurant, but Sydney wasn't sure. Sydney squinted her eyes to get a better view of the women, but she didn't want Jason to see her. As Sydney discreetly took two steps forward, the passenger nudged the driver, and it sounded like someone said, "Oh shit, go girl go!" The blue 2003 Grand Am Pontiac sped out of the parking lot and turned left onto Johnston Street. Sydney wasn't going to say anything to Jason, but she was more than sure the women had something to do with his flat tires. If the truth ever came out, she would still pretend like she didn't know anything.

***

Sydney sat at her desk while working on her weekly lesson plans. For the first time on a Monday, she wasn't ready to run out of the building. For some strange reason, the kids were calm today. Maybe it was the rain and cold front that entered the city last night. It was 3:45 pm and majority of her students were gone for the day. She was still at school because of a strange message she received through Facebook. An unacquainted woman said they needed to talk in person as soon as possible. Sydney wasn't down to meet the woman and laughed at the message. Once the woman said it was about Jason, Sydney agreed to meet her. She wasn't sure why the woman wanted to meet her, but she was tempted to find out why. Sydney had small feelings for Jason, but she still wanted to know what information about Jason was about.

"Did she get there yet?" Meeka asked. Her cell phone was pressed against her ear while she detangled Isabella's wet hair. She screamed and pulled away, which annoyed Meeka to her core.

"Obviously not if I'm still on the phone with you," Sydney joked.

"Damn bitch, excuse me." Meeka laughed. "I only asked a question, and I should have gotten a simple question."

"You know it's all love Meek Milly, but she needs to hurry up. I have things to do, and I'm ready for this tea!"

"What if she's his girlfriend and she's coming to confront you about being with her man?" Meeka asked.

"She better be ready to get carried out on a stretcher while I'm being escorted by the police department." She joked.

"Girl I bet Austin would LLOOOVEEEEE to see that. He probably would submit your photo for Donkey of the Day."

"Hell yea, I don't put anything past him anymore. It may just be me, but I haven't seen him in a while. I wonder what the hell he's up to."

"Awww, do you miss your hubby?" Meeka teased.

"You are funny Meeka, just plain ole funny. I'm trying to figure out if he's plotting something against us and what's his next move."

"I hope not, the last thing I need is him in my life. The next time I'm in close range with him I want to be standing over him. I'm going to be bare-faced with a .45 in my hand. I want him to see his killer before he enters the devil's pit."

"That sounds like music to my ears. Even though I haven't seen him in days, I'm still keeping my eyes on him."

"I'll be right behind you with my ears to the street. We can't get caught slipping right now. By the way, is he still calling your phone private?" Meeka asked.

"No, he isn't and thank God. The crazy part about this situation is that he never asks to see the boys. The last time he saw them was in the park with Xavier." Sydney said.

"Wait a minute, are you talking about when they got into that argument?" Meeka asked.

"Yes, ma'am that was the last time. You would think that would bother a parent, but not him."

"I guess we can rule him out as being a parent. I could never and would never go that long without seeing my baby girl." Meeka implied.

"My point exactly Meek, but I guess everyone isn't like us." Sydney shrugged her shoulders as if Meeka could see her.

"Well, maybe they should be. Whatever yall have going on shouldn't interfere with him seeing the boys. Just because you don't want him in your life as a husband, they still need him in their life as a father."

"I know all of that, and I have told him this on several occasions. None of that matters when you are trying harm their mother in every way possible. If he kills me or if I go to jail, I hope he doesn't think his getting my kids!"

"No Sydney, we are not going to have this conversation. We need to start plotting against him and clear that business. Maybe that will give you some kind of peace." Meeka said.

"Yes, it will. Oh my God Meek, I hate him!" Sydney whispered loudly. She was pissed just thinking about Austin and his no-good ways.

"Calm down Syd, don't get upset over this. It's going to get handled sooner than later, trust me. We just have to plot well before taking his ass out." Meeka said.

"I know, but thanks again for watching the boys last night. I needed that little outing even though it was ruined." Sydney said.

"You know everything is on the muscle. Besides, having the boys around means, I don't have to entertain Izzy all damn day. That girl would eat cake and play all day if she could." Meeka laughed.

"If I was in her shoes I would be the same way." Sydney laughed as well. She glanced at her wall clock and noticed it was 4:15 pm and the girl was late. She shook her head and continued writing.

"I have to go Sydney, someone is acting a fool," Meeka said.

"Okay girl, I'll see you at home, bye." Sydney removed the phone from her ear and ended the call. She thought about inboxing the woman, but she changed her mind. Sydney didn't want to come off as a stalker, but time was moving fast.

As she waited for the visitor to arrive, her mind raced like a Nascar. For hours Sydney investigated the woman's Facebook page, but she didn't find any valuable information. The profile picture was of the singer August Alsina, and the majority of the statuses were love, inspirational, and bible quotes. Sydney and the woman didn't have any mutual friends, and she was starting to think it was a fake profile. She wanted to call the woman and tell her don't come, but something told her not to do it.

Too many things were racing through her mind, but maybe the woman could clear her head.

Five minutes later, a knock at her classroom door pulled her from her lesson plans. Sydney dropped her pen and rushed to the little mirror she had nailed to her chalkboard. She figured it was the woman and she wanted to look decent before she opened the door.

Sydney feather her bangs out and dusted the lent off her blouse. Then she walked to the door and slowly opened it. Her eyes grew big when she saw that it was the pregnant woman from the restaurant. She didn't know what to say, but she gathered a few words and said, "It's you, what the hell!"

"Yes, it is me. Can I come in?" She asked.

"Are you the person I was talking to on Facebook?" Sydney asked, but she had a major attitude. If the woman replied yes, she would feel stupid and naïve. How could she not put the pieces together and figure out who was the woman she was talking too?

"Yes, I am. Can I still come in?" She asked and awkwardly smiled. She rubbed her perfect belly and played with her hem of her shirt while she waited for Sydney to respond. Sydney exhaled and dropped her head.

"How could I be this blind?" She said to herself and laughed. At first, she didn't want to let the woman enter her classroom, but she thought about it again and changed her mind. She opened the door wider and said, "Come in."

"Thank you," Sydney walked to her desk, and the woman entered the classroom. She closed the door and followed behind Sydney. Sydney sat at her desk and removed her glasses from her face. The woman didn't say much, but she was giving Sydney a headache already. Sydney rubbed her eyes and temples then she slid her glasses back onto her face.

"First let me introduce myself, my name is Jade Greene," Jade said.

"Hi Jade, I'm Sydney as you know and it's nice to meet you," Sydney said.

"It's nice to meet you as well."

"Enough of the small talk, what made you find me and come here today? First question is HOW did you find me?"

"When you told me to meet you at Grolee Elementary, I didn't think you was a teacher. You definitely don't look like a teacher," Jade slowly walked through the classroom and examined the handmade crafts the kids made. It seems like she was amazed by the kid's terrible handwriting and coloring projects.

"What's that supposed to mean?" Sydney asked.

"You look like you are a supermodel or video vixen." She laughed.

"I'm not sure if that's a compliment or an insult," Sydney replied.

"OH no, it's a compliment. I'm only trying to say you're beautiful Sydney, that's all."

"Oh okay, thank you."

"What is it like to be a teacher? I always wanted to be one, I wanted to teach first grade. If I wouldn't have dropped out of school in the 10th grade, I probably would be someone's favorite teacher now." She laughed again.

"You can always get your G.E.D. and go to college. Why not fulfill your dreams, you only live once baby," Sydney turned left and right in her rolling chair and tapped her coffin-shaped nails against the desk. The more she stared at Jade, her face became more familiar. Jade was the passenger who was trying to duck from her in the parking lot. Sydney wasn't ready to question Jade about that. She was going to wait until the conversation flowed then she would mention it.

"You're right about that, I have been thinking about it a lot lately. I'm twenty years old, I don't have a high school diploma, degree, I hardly have work history, and I'm pregnant with my second child. I need to get my life together for myself and for the sake of my kids. They can't grow up like me. I refuse to let that happen." Jade said.

"I feel you on that Jade. We all have to go hard for someone or something." Sydney said.

"You're right. Do you have a child or any kids?" Jade asked.

"Yes, I do have kids, three boys actually," Sydney turned her glass picture frame around and handed it to Jade. She grabbed the picture frame and stared at the pictures. She smiled for a second and returned the picture back to Sydney. Sydney didn't want to be rude, but she didn't stay late to make small talk or get well acquainted with Jade. She was ready to get the information she needed and continue with the rest of her day.

"The little one is your twin, but the other two must look like their father." She chuckled.

"You got that right they look exactly like their father." Sydney agreed.

"You have a beautiful family by the way. I bet everything is perfect in your life." She insisted.

"Everything is far from perfect in my life. I am currently going through a messy divorce with my husband and my relationship with my boyfriend is rocky right now."

"Damn," Jade said.

"I bet that shocked you. That's why you shouldn't judge a book by its cover." Sydney laughed.

"I guess I won't. I would never have expected that you were going through that."

"That means I don't look like what I'm going through." Sydney smiled and twirled her red pen.

Jade shook her head and said, "You don't at all."

"Okay, we know enough about one another. Why did you want to meet me?" Sydney asked.

"Right, uuummm, I'm not sure where to start."

"I know where you can start, was it you in that car last night?" Sydney asked.

"It was me, and I was the person who busted those tires," Jade rubbed her round belly and stared Sydney in the eyes. Sydney was shocked and didn't want to believe it, but her eyes told the truth. Sydney cleared her throat and removed her reading glasses from her face again. Then she exhaled and said, "Excuse me, what do you mean you busted those tires?"

"With all the strength I had, I slashed those tires like they were a piece of fruit. I'm sorry you had to get caught up in Jason's, and I mess. I just hate that bastard so much for everything he did to me. I would have slapped him in the restaurant, but he put a restraining order on me when I was ten weeks pregnant. That scary muthafucka makes me sick to my stomach."

"So you two do know one another?" Sydney asked.

"Yes, and we know each other very well. I've known Jason for a few years now." Jade said.

"Someone is lying, and I think it's you. I saw the way you were staring at us last night. You were obvious with your evil stares. I asked Jason if he knew you and he said he knew of you. He also said your name is Mariah and he only knew you from seeing you around town."

"Oh really, give me one second," Jade unzipped her purple wallet and searched for her license. Once she retrieved it, she handed it to Sydney. Sydney read the information, and in fact, her name was Jade and not Mariah. The city on the license read Abbeville so it made sense that she knew Jason. Sydney was shamed and embarrassed at the naïve words that she just said. She handed the license back to Jade and said, "Okay, your name is Jade Brossard, and you are from Abbeville, Louisiana, but that doesn't explain why you are here and how do you know Jason?"

"Look, I can sense the attitude in your voice, but I don't understand why?" Jade snapped.

"It's not attitude at all sweetheart. I'm only trying to figure out what's the meaning behind this meeting so I can go home. I'm starving, tired, and I'm ready to pull this wig off."

"Before I go on, I want to tell you something. I did not drive from Abbeville to Opelousas with a broken heater to be messy or start any confusion in your life. You and Jay seemed real cozy last night, and you almost looked like a couple in love. I've known Jason for a while, so I'm not surprised he said he didn't know me. If he didn't tell you he knew me, I can imagine what else he didn't tell you. I heard him say your name a few times, so I stayed up all night searching for you on Facebook. I wasn't sure if you knew the truth so I had to reach out. I can't let Jason play another woman how he played me without warning her. I'm a good person, and I can't have that on my heart." Jade said.

"All of that sounds nice, but how do you know Jason and what do you want from me? It's almost 5:00 pm and this conversation hasn't gotten anywhere. You are giving me a damn headache," Sydney closed her eyes and rubbed her temples.

Jade chuckled and said, "I know Jason because he is the father of my unborn child, but it's clear he didn't tell you that." Sydney felt a striking pain in her chest, but she played it cool. She replayed last night in her head, and everything started to make sense. Right now, she was feeling like a total dumbass for believing Jason and being an asshole toward Jade.

"Hold on a second, the baby in your stomach is Jason's? The Jason I was with last night?" Sydney asked.

"Yes, that Jason and I'm sorry you had to find out this way. It's kind of obvious that Jason hasn't told you much about himself."

"You can say that, but how do you know that?" Sydney asked.

"Because that's Jason and that's what makes him Jason. He's so damn secretive about everything, and I bet you haven't been to his house before." Sydney was surprised at what Jade said. The only thing she could do was shake her head in agreement and keep her ears open for the rest of the story.

"You hit it on the nose, but go on."

"Well, I met Jay three years ago at a birthday party. I had my eyes on him, and I thought he was cute, so I asked for his number. At the time, we were both super busy, so we hardly talked. After a while, I stopped calling him, and we lost contact. Somehow, we started communicating again, but it was nothing serious. A little over a year ago, we finally took it to another level, I was happy. I was crushing on Jason for a long time so within days I was going crazy over him. The first time we had sex, we didn't use protection, but I wanted to. I promise I wanted to, but I didn't want to ruin the moment. It did not bother him that was having unprotected sex. He said he was clean and he asked if I was. I told him yes. I'm always up to date on my HIV status and staying clear of any STD's. I'm not a sex-crazy girl, and I haven't had unprotected sex since I was with my child's father, but I still visit the clinic every six months. Jason and I had sex four times and on the third time is when I got pregnant. Around this time, Jason started acting funny, and we weren't spending time together like we use to. I asked him if he was getting cold feet about the baby and he said no, and that he's been busy. I brushed it off, but in my mind, I knew it was because of the baby. Now I'm thinking to myself like, I can't be a single mom of two. I considered having an abortion, but I changed my mind. I couldn't abort my baby because the dad was acting 'funny.' When it was time for my first appointment, he came with me. I can't lie, I was excited that he came and everything was back to normal. I actually started to think we would be a family and my oldest son would finally have a father or at least a father figure in his life."

"I hate to interrupt you, but what are you having now and how far are you?" Sydney asked.

"I am having a sweet baby girl, and I am naming her Meagan. I'm seven months pregnant, and I'm ready to pop. This little girl has given me acne from head to toe. In my first trimester, I had the worse morning sickness and constipation." She laughed.

"You sound like me when I was pregnant with my oldest son. That was my worse pregnancy out of all of them! My acne was so bad it looked like I was wearing a pepperoni pizza on my face. I didn't want to leave out the house." They both laughed.

"That was me last night. My sister literally dragged me out of the house by the arm. Besides doctor appointments and getting food, you will not see me outside. Society will not see me until this acne goes away. On top of that, my nose is getting wider by the day. Just give me a pair of glasses, a mustache, and you can call me Steve Harvey. My sister thinks I'm overacting, but all three of her pregnancies went smooth and did her body right. My second niece gave her booty, breast, and hips." She laughed.

"You and your sister sound like me and my best friend, Tameeka. She had a perfect glow while she was pregnant. She only gained twenty pounds, her hair and nails grew longer and stronger, and she did not have a touch of acne."

"Wow, I wish I could be her right now. Shit, how Jason fucked me up, I'll trade places with anyone right now. My baby and my life is ruined, and I can't do anything about it. How could I be so stupid over a guy again? You would think I learned at fourteen years old that niggas ain't shit," Jade dropped her head and sighed. Sydney could hear the sadness in Jade's voice, and she felt bad for her.

"I'm guessing Jason is denying the child now. You came here to tell me that and to thank you. Not many women would do something like that to help another sista out. I know it's tough out there being a young single mother, but you'll figure out. If you need any help with enrolling in school, please take down my number and call me," Sydney reached across the desk to give Jade a hug, but she didn't embrace Sydney. She slowly raised her head and stopped Sydney. Sydney was confused, but she didn't say anything. Sydney watched as the tears rolled down Jade's chubby cheeks and she rushed to grab the box of Kleenex. She handed it to Jade, and she pulled three of the soft tissues out. Jade wiped the tears away, but more came out. She sobbed harder, and Sydney ran to her side. She sat on the edge of the metal chair that Jade was sitting in and gave her a hug. She didn't know why Jade was crying, but right now she needed some love.

"Hey Jade, look at me, everything is going to be okay. You just have to trust in the Lord and believe that he will guide you out of this tangle of mess. How old are you by the way? If you're looking for a job, I can make a few phone calls. Most likely it's going to be a fast food job, but a job is a job."

"I'm twenty years old, but that's not the reason I came here. I came here to tell you that Jason is gay, undercover, and he also has HIV."

"EXCUSE ME! COME AGAIN! WHAT THE HELL DID YOU JUST SAY TO ME?" Sydney rose to her feet and stumbled backward. Sydney's reaction made Jade cry harder and snot bubbles formed in her nose.

"Please tell me you guys used a condom if you had sex?" Jade begged and blew her nose. Sydney tried to answer the question but instead dropped to the floor. She could no longer feel her legs, and the room started to spin. She didn't want to freak out like Meeka, did but it was hard not to. The information Jade dropped on Sydney was something serious and deadly.

"I – I – I – I don't remember Jade! Jason and I only had sex a few times and once without a condom. How could this happen, are you sure he's the one that gave it to you?" Sydney asked.

"Yes, I'm sure he's the one who gave it to me! Do you think I'm a hoe who sleeps around with just anyone? I know who gave me HIV and it's the same man you're sleeping with!" Jade shouted.

"No I don't think that, and I'm sorry if I offended you. I'm just appalled at everything you're saying to me.

Jason is such a sweet guy, how could he do something so vicious!?"

"That's the same thing I said. I didn't want to believe he gave it to me. For hours, I tried to convince myself that it was my fault, but it wasn't. When Jason decided to have sex with me unprotected he knew exactly what he was doing, but he didn't care. He did the same thing with you and no telling how many other girls. You, me and the rest of them are no different from one another. We all fell for the same line and good looks. If I could go back in time and not meet Jason, I swear I would. Every day I dread having this baby, and that hurts me to my core."

"Why?"

"Because my one dumb decision has ruined my child's life. How do you sit a child down and tell her that she was born with HIV? I can only prepare for the hate she's going to have towards me, but I have to accept it." She said. Every word Jade said made Sydney's stomach ache a little more, and her head throb a little harder. She tried to stand to her feet, but it felt like gravity was holding her back. Sweat formed on her forehead, so she used her shirt to wipe it away. She wanted to be angry, but she also wanted to be sad. In this moment, Sydney wasn't sure how to feel. She didn't have the right to only be upset at Jason, Sydney was also angry with herself. She knew the consequences of having unprotected, but Sydney didn't think it would happen to her like this.

"Jason swears to God he didn't give me HIV, but he is the person that did. For the first appointment, my doctor called me and said I needed to come in for my results. I begged them to tell me over the phone because I didn't have transportation, but they refused to. After searching for a ride for an hour, I finally made it to my doctor. He told me my child, and I have HIV, but I came in the Acute stage of it. As long as I take care of myself, I can live for however long the good Lord lets me."

"Does anyone in your family know you have it?" Sydney's headache began to fade away, and she was now able to stand to her feet. Like a crab, she walked to the nearest desk and maneuvered her wide hips into it. She was uncomfortable in the tiny desk, but she didn't care. She was just glad she was able to get off the floor without having to calling 9-1-1.

"No one knows yet, and I'm not sure how to tell them. Once I have Meagan, and they see which floor I'm on in the hospital, they might put the pieces to the puzzle together. If not, I'll be a woman and tell them what happened."

"This is unreal. How does a twenty-year-old tell her mother she has HIV," Sydney covered her wrinkled lips with her hands and whimpered. Not only was she crying for herself, she was crying for Jade as well.

"I'm not sure how I'm going to do that, but I have a few more months to figure it out. I want to hide it from everyone forever, but I know I can't. We're a close family, and I owe them the truth." Jade said.

"You are too young for this Jade. Way too fucking young. DO YOU HEAR ME? A person your age should be in college stressing about finals, term papers, online quizzes, and enjoying their twenties. They aren't talking about their status. I'm so sorry you have to go through this."

"You're right, and how things are going in my life, I'm not sure if I will ever be that person," Jade said.

"Don't say that you can still be that person," Sydney said.

"I don't see it happening, and I'm okay with that. You don't have to be sorry for anything, you aren't the person who ruined my life Jason is. Instead of facing his problem he moved away."

"He told me he moved here to be closer to his grandmother," Sydney said.

"Jason is a liar, his grandmother died of colon cancer seven years ago."

"I guess everything that came out of his mouth was a lie. What if I have…HIV, what AM I going to do? What am I going to tell him, friends and family? My sons need me. They need their mother in their lives!! I am all they have, and they can't lose me, they can't! What am I going to tell my boyfriend?"

"You have a boyfriend?" Jade asked.

"Yes, I have a boyfriend, but we're kind of a break right now. That doesn't matter though, I still love him."

"I'll tell you like the doctor told me, it's not the end of the word, and life goes on. Now, this is ME talking, GO GET YOURSELF CHECKED! If you need anything, call me, please," Jade reached for Sydney's phone and programmed her number. Sydney didn't move or say anything. It was like her body was frozen.

***

It was 8:30 pm and Sydney finally made it home. After leaving the clinic, she decided to find the nearest bar and drank all her feelings away. With a heavy vomit smell on her clothes and shoes, Sydney stumbled into the house and slammed the door. No one was home, and Sydney was glad. With her results in one hand a bottle of whiskey in the other hand, Sydney walked into the laundry room and peeled the smelling clothes off. The chunky vomit covered her hair and made her gag several times. She dropped the bottle and paper on the dryer then she ran to the sink. The vomit pushed out, and she couldn't stop it. Her throat was on fire, and the gagging caused stomach pains.

"OH, my Go..." Sydney couldn't finish her sentence because the vomit continued to pour out. She felt terrible, but she didn't regret getting drunk. After a day like today, she had every right to get wasted.

Once the vomit stopped coming out of her mouth, she turned the hot water on and grabbed the dish detergent. She squeezed a large amount into the sink and began to rinse the sink out. After she was done, she placed her head under the faucet and filled her mouth with warm water. Sydney gurgled and swished them around her mouth, then she released the water into the sink. She could feel a hangover approaching, and she knew she would have to call in sick tomorrow. School was the last thing she wanted to think about. Making her way upstairs without tumbling down was the first and only thing she was concerned with.

Sydney walked to the fridge to grab the bowl of green grapes, but she stopped before she opened the fridge. She forgot she was only wearing a bra and thong and needed to change fast. As she wobbled to the laundry room, she held onto the countertop and used her free hand to rub her forehead. Once she made it to the laundry room, she grabbed her paper with her test results and raised it in the air. Sydney struggled to keep her heavy eyes open while she read the results again. Seeing that she was HIV negative took major stress off her shoulders, but she also felt bad. While she was celebrating, Jade was probably at home contemplating on how she would tell her family about her status.

Sydney pictured Jade's sad eyes in her head and sighed. She couldn't get over how much Jade was facing at such a young age.

"I hate you Jason, and I hope you die!" Sydney banged her opened hands against the dryer and shouted. Every time she thought about Jason, a wave of rage surged through her body. She tried her best to block everything out of her head, but she couldn't. The betrayal was fresh, and it would take time for the pain to go away.

Meeka walked into the house and leaned against the door. Sydney was startled, but she quickly covered her body and turned around. When she noticed it was Meeka she sighed and said, "You scared me, I thought you were Hustle."

"No, it's me, I told him to take the boys to the grocery store with him."

"Oh okay, thanks."

"Don't mention it, but are you drunk? I can smell the brown liquor from here," Meeka flared her nose to inhale the smell and walked to Sydney. Sydney pointed to the bottle of Whiskey and shook her head.

"I went to the bar when I left the clinic, but this was the drink for the ride home." Sydney could hardly stand straight or keep her eyes open while she talked to Meeka. She didn't like Meeka seeing her like this, but this time she didn't care.

"You should have called me to pick you up. I know today was.....overwhelming, but driving while drinking isn't cool Syd. You could have hurt yourself or someone else." Meeka said.

"No, what isn't cool is Jason's careless ways," Sydney grabbed the bottle, but Meeka grabbed it from her and walked into the kitchen. She placed the bottle in the sink's cabinet and reentered the laundry room. Then she opened the dyer and grabbed Sydney's a t-shirt and a pair of red jogging shorts. She smelled Sydney's hair and jumped back. The odor was loud, and Meeka couldn't tolerate it for long. She took a few steps backward and leaned her back on the countertop.

"You might want to wash your hair before you get in bed."

"I will and if I had the energy to wash my whole body I would." She laughed. Meeka smiled, but she didn't laugh. She had various questions for Sydney, but she wasn't sure where to start or how to approach the conversation.

"Are you going to work tomorrow?" Meeka asked.

"No, I'm not. I may take the rest of the week off. I need to clear my head, and I can't face Jason in that environment." Sydney said.

"I feel you on that and take all the time you need to clear your head. You had a rough day today Sydney."

"Shit, who are you telling! I'm still shocked at all this. Jason is a professional at hiding the truth, that dirty muthafucka!"

"Did you talk to him about it?" Meeka asked.

"As soon as I left the clinic I called his trifling ass. At first, he tried to deny it, but once I gave him the facts he gave in."

"So, is it true, does he have HIV?" Meeka asked.

Sydney sighed and nodded her head. Meeka smacked her lips and dropped her head. She was praying that it wasn't true and all of this was a big confusion.

"Yep, it is true, and he told me everything. He at least owed me that for putting my life and health in jeopardy," Sydney leaned forward and pushed against the wall. She started to cry and banged against the wall.

"What all did he say?" Meeka asked.

"Just like Philly, Jason is in the closet, and only a few people know. When he was eighteen years old, he met a guy from Mississippi on a dating website. Within a month, he fell in love with him. The guy's name was Pauly Deans, and he was twenty-five years old. No one knew he was dating the guy so he would secretly meet him in Mississippi and sometimes in Louisiana.   Jason said everything was going well between the two, but suddenly, Pauly disappeared."

"What do you mean he disappeared?" Meeka asked.

"Pauly stopped answering his calls, text messages, and he deleted his account on the dating website. For weeks, he cried, but he got over it. Around that time his former high school was hosting a blood drive, and he decided to donate blood. The workers had to pull him to the side and let him know that they couldn't use his blood and why."

"Oh my God, no!" Meeka gasped and covered her mouth. The story was becoming intense and heart filling. She wasn't sure if she could handle any more of it, but she had to hear the ending.

"He didn't believe it when they told him at the blood drive, so he went to the clinic. First, he was tested by saliva, and the results were negative. He wanted to be sure, so he made them test him by blood. The blood result came back positive, and he said he felt his world tumble in his lap. Could you imagine getting that kind of news at that age? I'm surprised he didn't kill himself. I know I would have."

"I'm pretty sure Jade knows how he felt. It was like history repeated itself and I don't feel sorry for him. I feel sorry for that little girl, she's so young. I need a sit, a pill, and a drink after hearing this story. Is this the end or is there more, please tell me there isn't more?" Meeka walked to the dryer and sat on top of it. She dropped her head and stared at her lap. Sydney walked to the dryer and stood next to Meeka and said, "No, it isn't the end Meek it's a little more to it."

"Like what?"

"Last year at Myrtle Beach, he saw the guy, but he didn't recognize Jason. He said he looked a little different, but not much. The fact that he continued with his life like nothing happened pissed Jason off. He promised himself that every person he crossed paths with sexually had to feel his pain. That makes Jason selfish on so many levels. You know what's crazy, he never apologized to me. Something in my heart tells me he's going to quit teaching at Grolee, move out of Opelousas, and do the exact same thing to another woman. Running from his problems with Jade is why he moved here, but that's not what he told me. He said he moved here to be closer to his grandmother." Sydney said.

"Why didn't Jade press charges on him or tell anyone?" Meeka asked.

"No one in her family knows she has HIV and she plans to keep it that way until she has the baby. She's even thinking about not telling anyone until she dies."

"What do you mean until she dies?" Meeka asked.

"Just speaking in general Meeka, calm down."

"I don't even want to hear the word death or die come out of your mouth. I'm trying to wrap my head around this, but I can't. It's a lot to process Syd, I can't lie. It had to be Santana watching over you while you had sex with Jason. You dodge a major bullet girl, let's be thankful for that."

"I know, but if I would have contracted the virus, it would have been in the early stage of it. That's why when

Jason was tested by saliva his results were negative. It's called the acute stage actually."

"Wwwooooowwwww, I never knew that. I trust Hustle and all that good shit, but this is making me want to get tested." Meeka said.

"You should do that. You have the right to know your status."

"I'm going to the clinic tomorrow, things can happen too fast. Have you spoken to Jade yet? I know she would happy to hear your results." Meeka said.

"I haven't called her yet, and I probably won't call her until tomorrow. I feel like crap, and I'm ready to wash my hair then get in bed."

"I think you should call her tonight and let her know. She deserves to know as well Sydney."

"I hate to admit it, but you're right. After I wash my hair, I'll call her, but hopefully, she isn't sleeping. You know you never wake a pregnant woman up out of her sleep." Sydney laughed.

"I wish someone would have told Brink's ass that when I was pregnant. He caught a few punches to the ribs for that bullshit." Meeka laughed and waved her hand to motion Sydney to follow her upstairs. Sydney laughed, but she also cried. She wished that she could wake up tomorrow and none of this happened.

They walked into the bathroom, and Meeka closed the door. She on the toilet and stared at the white wall. She still had a lot she needed to say to Sydney, but she didn't want to offend her. She didn't want to make her cry more, but everything on her heart had to be said.

"I swear Meek the only thing I thought about was my kids. If I would have d-i-e-d, Austin would not get my kids. I would rather them in foster care instead of in his care."

"I know today was a lot to deal with and handle. I bet waiting for those results felt like your entire life flashed before your eyes. I'm sorry you had to go through this, but you know I'm here to help you get through this. If something would ever happen to you, Austin would have to fight me to get those kids."

"Do you mean that Meek?" Sydney asked.

"Hell yea I do. I love them like they are mine. What Jason did was fucked up, but don't let that bring you down. You are good, and you'll get past this. Look at it as a lesson learned and put him in the past."

"I wish I could delete him from my memory man. To think I was giving Xavier the cold shoulder because I wanted Jason. That was stupid of me, but I wish someone would have told me to catch my head," Sydney removed the rest of her clothing from her body and adjusted the hot and cold water. She waited a few seconds before stepping into the shower because she wanted to make sure the water was warm. Meeka opened the cabinets and grabbed a bottle of Suave shampoo and conditioner, then she handed the bottle to Sydney. She didn't waste any time squeezing a large amount of shampoo into the palm of her hand and lathering it into her wet hair. The smell of vomit began to fade away, and the sweet smell of lavender took over her body and hair.

"I tried telling you baby girl, but you didn't want to listen. As always, people must see some things for themselves. Now that you're done with Jason, what are you going to do with Xavier? Are you going to tell him about what happened with Jason?" Meeka asked.

"I'm going to work on my relationship like I should have done since day one. I thought about telling him about Jason, but I decided not to. I don't think there is any reason to tell him. We all know Jason won't open his damn mouth!"

"Hmmm, you got that right girl. He's taking his dirty little secrets to the graveyard."

"I'm not sure if I should be upset or sad with him. Meeka, one wrong move could have caused me my life, and that's crazy! I wish you would have told me to leave his pretty ass where I found him. How could I be so stupid," Sydney repeatedly slapped her forehead with her wet towel. Meeka stood to her feet and grabbed the towel out of her hand. She wrapped her arms around Sydney and gave her a hug. She didn't care that her body was soaked and soapy. By the way, Sydney was sobbing and crying Meeka knew she needed a hug and her friend by her side.

"It's okay Sydney, let it all out. It doesn't matter if you're right or wrong, I'm behind you a hundred percent."

"Tell me something Meeka, when did our lives get so fucked up like this?" Sydney cried out.

"I can tell you the exact day it did, and every time I think about it, it makes me sick to my stomach. It had to be one of the worse days of my lives. I can still hear the recording in my head."

Meeka sat low in the unmarked car and patiently waited for Wendell to arrive. Wendell was a twenty-two-year-old rookie on the police force. He also worked for Meeka as well, but no one knew. Not even his girlfriend, family, or friends. His job didn't pay him nearly what Meeka paid him, but he still loved his job. When Meeka approached him about working with her, he didn't hesitate jumping on payroll. Meeka knew he wouldn't say no for the simple fact he was a starving rookie.

"Where are you Wen?" Meeka stared and tapped on the window. It was a little foggy, but she still managed to see. Between the low temperature and rain, Meeka was slightly annoyed with Wendell's tardiness. She told him to arrive at 4:45 am, but it 5:30 am. The temperature was in the high 30's, and the rain was slowly increasing. Meeka was ready to get back into her bed and catch up on some sleep. In the past week, she could count on one hand how many hours of sleep she had. She was glad they slept at the house on Sonny Street and didn't have to drive far to get home.

Ten minutes later Meeka spotted a bright red pickup truck approaching her car. She waited until Wendell was closer to her car before she got out. She used her hands to cover her hair and got into his truck. She dapped him and said, "What up fool?"

"Shit Meek, just chilling. I'm sorry I took longer, but I have some crazy information for you."

"Oh Lord, is it that bad? Lord knows I can't handle any worse news or bullshit." Meeka roughly rubbed her bare face and leaned her head against the window. Wendell reached under his seat and pulled out a small voice recorder.

"I'll let you be the judge of that." Wendell pressed the red play button and placed the recorder on the seat. As the voices grew louder, Meeka's hurt dropped. It was Justice and Austin, and she could feel that the conversation between them was going to get crazy.

"Look Juju, all you have to do is testify against Tameeka and Sydney it's not that big of a deal like you're making it sis."

"I don't know Austin. I can give you some people out of the Oil Mill that works for Meeka. I can give you Marlo or Hustle. They hold just as much weight in the game." Justice said.

"NO, I DON'T WANT ANY OF THEM! I WANT THOSE BITCHES ON A SILVER PLATTER!" Austin shouted.

"Austin, it isn't that easy, and you know that. You know how Meeka moves. I swear she has eyes and ears everywhere. She probably has ears in this interrogation room. Don't sleep on Sydney because she's the same way. You would think Meeka carried her for nine months and birthed her!" Justice said.

"Come on now Juju. You're being a little past dramatic." Austin said and slammed his hands on the table.

"No, I'm not! If I testify against them, Meeka will kill me or get me killed. I've seen Meeka in action and I know for a fact death would be my only way out."

"What kind of things have you seen her do?" Austin asked.

"Right now, that doesn't matter."

"You're right we'll get back to that later. You need to stop overthinking this situation and listen to me. If you *testify, we will put you in The Witness Protection Program. Your identity and everything will change, and you have to lose contact with everyone you know."*

"Not no, but hell to the no! I'm not going through all of that just to help you get revenge on Meek and Sydney."

"It's not revenge it's getting two people off the streets. This is my job, and I'm also trying to save your ass because you are family, my sister to be exact. If you don't switch sides, you'll be going down with them. I have no choice Juju."

"You really don't have anything on us but the rumors you have heard through the streets." Justice rolled her eyes and turned away. Austin grabbed her by the shoulders and made her face him. She was a little scared, but she didn't show any emotion.

"Oh, is that so?" Austin smirked and asked.

"Yea, that's 'so' my nigga."

"Right before Glenn mysteriously committed suicide he told me a few things," Austin said.

"Like what?"

"I know all about him working as a male escort in White Castle, Baton Rouge, Opelousas, and Franklin. My WIFE is a high paid hoe that I knew nothing about. Oh, yea, thank you for telling me that. I thought it was family over everything, but I guess I was wrong." Austin said.

"Hey, don't blame me. I thought you knew she was a hoe." Justice laughed.

"No, I sure didn't. I thought she just did a little stripping on the side."

"You were stupid for even thinking that. She does wwayyyyy more on the side." Justice turned away and mumbled.

"How could she be so low down and dirty?! That is my wife and the mother of my kids! I'm married to a paid hoe Justice. Do you know how that shit feels? No, you don't!"

"Watch your mouth. The correct term is escort."

"An escort and hoe is the same thing if you ask me." Austin laughed.

"See that's the reason why she is leaving your ass. You are so close-minded."

"She's leaving me because of that bitch Tameeka."

"Okay Austin, whatever you say. I honestly can't get on a stand Austin, I'm sorry. If you love me like you say you do you wouldn't let me get tied up in all of this mess."

"If YOU love yourself you wouldn't get tied into this mess. Do you know what kind of charges Meeka can get hit with? Distributing cocaine, conspiracy, prostituting, running an organized crime and the list goes on. Just imagine how embarrassed the entire family would be. You are so innocent in grandpa's eyes. Picture his reaction when your face is all over the news." Justice stood to her feet and paced through the room. She had a clear view of her family in her head, and it wasn't good.

"Okay, I'll do it." She mumbled.

"What?" He smiled and laughed.

"I said I'll do it, but what exactly am I doing?" She asked.

"Instead of testifying I have a better idea, an idea that won't get you killed," Austin said.

"Okay, let me hear it."

"All you have to do is plant a few microphones in her house and wear a mic at all times. With that evidencee, you won't have to take the stand."

"Is that it?" Justice asked.

"Yea that's it. I told you I would save you, but you must help me a little. I got you, sis, don't I always?"

"Yea you do, but my name can't come up at all!!" Justice said.

"I promise it won't. So are you down?" Austin asked.

Justice exhaled and said, "Yea I'm down."

Good, I'm going to get the microphones today and hit you up. We're going to meet outside of Opelousas. I don't want anyone to see us together anymore. I want everyone to think that we aren't on speaking terms."

"Okay." Wendell stopped the tape, but he didn't say anything. Meeka could feel she was getting sick, so she opened the door wide. She held her stomach and began to gag. Shortly after that, vomit began to rush out of her mouth. She tried to collect herself, but the vomit continued to come out.

"Oh shit, let me get you a bottle of water." Wendell reached to the back seat and grabbed a bottle of Fiji water. He handed it to Meeka, but she stopped him. The vomit didn't stop; it ran like a faucet. She started to cry, and her tears were at the same pace with her vomit.

"Tameeka are you okay? Do I need to call you an ambulance?"

"No Wen, I'm good, but thanks. Where is that bottle of water and do you have a napkin or something that I can wipe my face with?" Wendell shook his head and handed Meeka the bottle. Then he reached into his pocket for his handkerchief and gave it to Meeka. She popped the cap off the water and took a big gulp. Then she patted her face and took another sip of the water.

"Are you sure? I haven't seen anyone vomit like that ever."

"I'm good, that recording caught me off guard. When did you get this?" Meeka asked.

"A few minutes ago that's why I was late. What I originally had was some information about Philly." Wendell said.

"Oh yea, what kind of information?" Meeka took a sip of water and swished it around her mouth. A few seconds later she spit the water out and closed the door. The bottle of water was nearly empty, but she still held onto it.

"In a week Philly is planning to flee the country. We're not sure where he's going or where he's currently hiding, but if this reliable source comes through, we'll know all of that." Meeka smiled to herself, but she wanted to laugh. Rocko was the reliable source that called into Crime Stoppers and gave the fake tip. She thought Wendell had some valuable information, but it was only her own information.

"Wow, that's crazy. I hope they catch him before he flees because if they don't, he's going to get away forever."

Meeka said. She was ready to end this conversation and go home.

"Trust me Tameeka the authorities are working on this case."

"I believe you, but can I have the recorder?" She asked.

"Of course," Wendell handed Meeka the recorder. She dapped him down and said, "Thank you Wen, but I have to go. I'll fuck with you later."

"Okay." Meeka rushed out of the car and got into her car. She was so destroyed. She wasn't sure if she could drive home without wrecking. Sydney and Meeka always suspected Justice to be a snake, but they never had any proof. To hear everything Justice said was mind-blowing.

"I can't believe someone would put your life and health in danger like that. I know I said it already, but it's still shocking to me! I swear when I see him I'm going to rock out. They might call me Marlo Mike or Mad Max when I'm done with him." Meeka said.

"Let him find someone else's life to ruin. Don't even get your hands dirty with him," Sydney turned the shower off, and Meeka handed her a big blue towel. She rubbed the towel against her body and hair then she stepped out of the shower. The humidity had Meeka covered in sweat, so she opened the door and leaned against the wall. As Sydney used the towel to dry her hair more, Meeka stood quietly. Somehow, she felt this problem was created because of her, and she had to resolve it her way.

"I don't want to hear that Syd. I lost Santana because of a trifling ass nigga, I can't lose you either."

"If I would have had HIV Meek I wouldn't have died! Listen to what I'm saying and let it ride, okay?"

"I hear you, Syd, I hear you loud and clear," Meeka said.

"Good, I'm going to bed, my head is banging girl."

Sydney grabbed the black rubber band and pulled her damp hair into a tight ponytail. Meeka nodded her head, but she ignored everything Sydney said. If she saw Jason anywhere, he had some explaining to do to her and the cold steel she would have on her hip.

Chapter 4 January 2017

Meeka and Sydney pulled in the driveway staring at the strange car parked in her driveway. Tori's car was also parked there, which made Meeka roll her eyes. This would be her first time seeing or even speaking to Tori since the argument. Part of her was glad that Tori was here because that meant Hustle is speaking to his mother again. The other part of her was annoyed that she was there because Meeka wasn't in the mood to argue with her or anyone else.

After a few weeks of being depressed, Sydney was back to her old self. Just as she suspected, Jason quit his job, and she hadn't seen or heard from him since their dinner date last month. Since she met Jade, they have kept in touch at least three times a week. Sydney took the liberty of helping Jade enroll into an online GED program, and she also helped her find a job. She was amazed at how Jade wasn't depressed and always kept a positive attitude about her situation. Sydney could admit if she was Jade, she would be the total opposite. A small portion of Sydney felt guilty that she dodged the virus and Jade didn't.

"Girl, that Zumba class has my legs killing me," Sydney smacked her lips and rubbed the back of her legs. Meeka handed her a bottle of room temperature water and said, "Here, drink some water, water fixes everything."

"I should have poured holy water on my life a few months ago. Maybe it would have been fixed." She laughed and exited the car. Sydney twisted the cap off the water bottle and swallowed two big gulps. She was breathing heavy and needed to lie down. Her entire body was sore, and she was regretting that she followed Meeka to the gym.

"I'm serious, Meek, and I think I need a massage." As Sydney got out of the car, she held her lower back and carefully walked behind Meeka. Meeka rolled her eyes and tossed her head back. Sydney burst into laughter and started to walk straight.

"Stop complaining, girl. It's all going to be worth it. If we stay on this no carb diet and workout three times a week, we'll be back to our pre-pregnancy bodies."

"Girl, bye, that body left the building years ago," Sydney stared at her body, but Meeka rolled her eyes and continued walking up the driveway. Sydney wasn't a size four like she was years ago, but her body was still amazing. Women would pay for the small waistline and thick thighs she has.

"Whatever, Sydney, Xavier isn't complaining and neither should you."

"He was so desperate to get me back, he wouldn't complain about anything." She laughed.

"You're right about that. I'm glad you two are working things out."

"I can't lie, I'm glad we're working things out as well. Now that I'm thinking with my head and not my pussy, I missed Xavier a lot. I hope this is the last time he and I go through something like this." Sydney replied.

"It better be, or I'm going to knock his ass out. He'll be laid out flat on his back."

"Damn, Meek, on his back?" Sydney asked and laughed.

"Hell yea, he'll be flat on his pockets." Meeka and Sydney laughed. Even though Sydney and Xavier weren't officially back together, she was back in the house. She knew eventually with time and great effort, they would be back to the happy couple they once were. She still hadn't told him about Jason or the HIV scare, and she planned to keep it that way. It was no need to get him in his feelings about nothing. However, without letting him know why she did ask him to get tested.

"See that's why I fuck with you, Meek. Right or wrong you always have my back."

"That's what friends are for. Now let me get in my house and see who this strange car belongs to," Meeka and Sydney walked into her home and found Hustle, his mom, Isabella, and an unknown man sitting on the couch. Hustle locked eyes with Meeka, but she couldn't figure out the blank stare on his face. He sat far from his mom and the man, but for some reason, they looked like a happy couple. The man resemblance Hustle in various ways; his hair texture, facial structure, and body frame. While playing with Isabella's hand, Tori smiled at Meeka and said, "Hello Tameeka, you're finally back.

"Hi and yea, Zumba lasted a little longer today."

"Who is that and why is he holding Izzy?" Sydney whispered into Meeka's ear as she closed the door. The man bounced Isabella on his knee, and they both laughed. She interacted with him as is she knew him all her life. Meeka was a little uncomfortable with him holding Isabella, but she going to find out who this man was.

"I don't know, but I'm about to find out."

"Brink, baby, introduce your dad to your girlfriend. Brink Senior, she's also Isabella's mom," Tori smiled and pointed to Meeka. Meeka was surprised at how nice Tori was being to her. She wasn't sure if it was sincere of it she was putting on an act in front of Brink Senior.

"Did you say Brink Senior, as in Brink's dad because he's a junior?" Meeka nearly fainted because of the words she was hearing. Besides seeing a few pictures of Brink Senior, this was Meeka's first time seeing him in person. He didn't look like an addict or anyone who did drugs. His gray hair indicated he was older, but he looked good for his age. He basically looked like an older version of Hustle. That assured Meeka that Hustle would still look great once he got older and grew gray hair.

"That is usually how that works. Right, Isabella, that's usually how that works." He laughed and planted a kiss on Isabella's neck. She snorted and giggled loudly. Meeka laughed as well, she has never seen Isabella so tickled before.

"Ummm, I'm sorry dad, this is my girlfriend Isabella, I mean Tameeka. Tameeka, this is my dad Brink," Hustle stood to his feet and walked to Meeka. Then he grabbed her hand and led her to his dad. Hustle's hands were sweaty and shaky, but Meeka could understand why. Brink hadn't seen his dad in ten years, and she thought more time would have gone by without him seeing his dad.

"Hi, it's nice to finally meet the Senior. Brink, you didn't tell me you looked EXACTLY like your father. Now I see where he gets his good looks from." Everyone laughed expect Hustle. He smiled and raised his eyebrows. Something told Meeka that Hustle was uncomfortable and wasn't feeling this conversation. She stroked his arm then she placed her head on it. Brink Senior stared Meeka up and down, but she tried not to make eye contact with him. Her eyes were glued to Hustle, and she was trying to find answers within his eyes. She couldn't though, his eyes were blank, and his vibe towards his dad was a little cold. If Hustle had any animosity towards his dad, he had every right to. On the other hand, Meeka could see Tori hadn't taken her eyes off Brink Senior, which was strange. A smile was stuck on her face as if she was glad to see and reunite with him.

Everyone was wearing a different emotion on their sleeve, and it was making Meeka's head spin.

"Yes, I'm where he gets his good looks from and not his mom." Brink Senior laughed.

"Oh, whatever, Brink," Tori slapped Brink Senior on the leg and began to blush. He turned to her and laughed. Even when he turned away, she was still smiling at him. Hustle looked over his shoulder and gave his mom a funky look. She ignored Hustle and continued to stare at her husband. Meek laughed to herself because it reminded her of how she stared at Hustle. She wondered if she looked that thirsty as well.

"I'm only kidding, but who is this pretty lady at the door?" Brink Senior pointed at Sydney and Meek said, "This is my best friend, Sydney."

"Hi it's nice to meet you," Sydney walked closer and extended her hand out to Brink Senior. He gently shook it then everyone sat down. For a minute, no one said anything. Tori and Brink Senior sat closely and played with Isabella. Hustle sat low in the couch staring at the television. A commercial for cookware was playing, and he seemed interested, or that was his way to ignore his parents. Sydney scrolled down her Instagram timeline, and Meeka tried to figure out a way to break the silence.

"Mr. Brink, this is an unexpected visit, when did you get in town?" Meeka asked.

"I got in town last night, but Tori and I wanted to surprise Junior." He said.

"My name is Brink, dad, we have the same name." Brink snapped, and Meeka laughed. With his arms folded across his chest and his tight mouth, he was acting like a child.

"Baby what's with the attitude?" Meeka asked.

"Yes, baby, what's with the attitude?" Tori asked.

"No attitude, I'm going into the kitchen. Does anyone want anything?" Brink asked.

"I'll take a bottled of water son." Brink Senior said.

"Okay, anyone else want anything?"

"No." Tori and Sydney said.

"I'll go with you, baby, we'll be right back," Meeka grabbed Hustle's hand, and they stood to their feet. She sped out of the living room so they could make it into the kitchen fast. Once they made it into the kitchen, Hustle leaned against the high countertop and exhaled. His back was faced to Meeka, and he stared out of the window. The thought of his father being in his house and his presence at the same time had his vibe on a thousand.

"Isabella has only known your dad for a few minutes, and she's in love with him already. Let me find out she thinks that's you." Meeka laughed and walked to the fridge. Then she moved the gallon of milk to the left and grabbed the wide Fiji bottle of water. She handed it to Hustle and closed the fridge. He shook his head, and he started to laugh.

"I may look like him, but I DON'T act like him. We are two different people, and I want everyone to know that!!!"

"Brink, calm down, I know you're not your father. NO one is comparing you and your father's characteristics. If you were like him, I would have beaten your ass a long time ago." Meeka laughed.

"I'm not him, and I won't ever be like him. He's not a man, and I'm a man!"

"Baby, sssshhhhhhh, like I said, calm down. Once again, no one is comparing you to him. Why didn't you tell me your dad and mom was coming here? I would have cooked and clean, you know your mom says she can smell the germs as soon as she walks in." Meeka laughed.

"I didn't tell you because I didn't know Tameeka, I'm sorry. My parents arrived about ten minutes ago. I wanted to call you." Hustle said.

"It's okay hunny, but what's up with you. You seem a little......thrown off by your father's presence."

"I am, and it's not only that, my mom is acting weird. It's like she's happy to see my dad or something." Hustle said.

"Maybe she is Brink, but you can't be upset about that. Legally that still is her husband, so she's a little happy to see her old boo thang. Besides, he is handsome and you two look just alike. I know if I hadn't seen you in a while, I would stare like that also," Meeka rubbed her hands against Hustle's back and laughed. She tried to make him laugh, but it didn't work much. Hustle was pissed, and it wasn't a lot that could change the way he felt.

"How could she be happy to see this clown? After all the bull shit he has put her and me through, she has no reason to even talk to him!!"

"Calm down, baby, don't get yourself upset because of them, it's not worth it," Meeka said.

"I know it isn't, but I'm so pissed right now. She's staring at him like he's the next best thing since slice bread. She's such a dumb ass, and if she wasn't my mom, I probably would smack the shit out of her."

"Oh my God, Hustle, that's deep, don't you think?" Meeka asked. Hustle's words surprised her. She never heard him speak about his mother in this manner. He slowly exhaled and turned around. He stared into Meeka's eyes then he kissed her chin. Within seconds Hustle was calmed, and she was glad.

"It is and my bad, let's go back in the living room. I'm ready for them to get the hell out of my house." He chuckled.

"You and me both, I love you baby."

"I love you too, Meek." Tameeka and Hustle reentered the living room she was praying he had a different attitude towards his parents. He handed his dad the bottle of water, then he sat down. Meeka reached for Isabella, and she jumped into Meeka's arms. Everyone laughed expect Hustle. Meeka slightly rolled her eyes because she knew Hustle still had his attitude.

"That is one beautiful baby you two have created. I hope I'm getting a grandson soon." Brink Senior smiled.

"Yes sir, but in due time, we aren't getting any younger," Meeka said and laughed.

"I understand that, but don't wait too long."

"You got that right, but we want to be more settled for another child. Isabella caught us by surprise, but we're grateful for her." Meeka said.

"Tameeka, you have such a lovely home for a young woman. If you don't mind me asking, what is your occupation? I know it cost a pretty penny to keep this place running and in order." Brink Senior chuckled and asked.

"I wouldn't consider my age young, but I'm a stay at home mom."

"Oh, really and that pays the bills?" Brink Senior smiled, but Meeka wasn't sure if he was being sarcastic or truthful. Either way, she wasn't going to tell him the truth about her occupation and lifestyle.

"Yes, it does." Meeka gave Brink Senior a wide, but fake smile. Meeka was sure that Tori had filled him in on what Meeka's occupation was. She was also sure that she skipped the part about her son being a drug dealer.

"I'm tired of the small talk." Hustle interrupted.

"Brink stop," Meeka snapped.

"Be quiet Tameeka, I have too much on my heart. Dad, why are you her and be real for once in your life?"

"Junior, what do you mean why am I here?" He asked.

"I guess that dope fried your brain to your skull so I'll break down for you. I haven't seen you in ten years, and the last time I checked, you lived in Monroe, Louisiana. I'm not sure where you live in Monroe, but I do know that much. There is a reason you are here, and it's not just some reason. It's a legit reason so tell me right now what it is!!"

"Brink, your father is here to talk you. We have some important and exciting news to tell you."

"What kind of news mom, since you're so excited to see him. Dad, are you still on that shit?" Hustle asked.

"What?"

"I guess you're hard of hearing, I asked are you still on that shit?"

"I think you need to watch how you speak to me. I know things aren't great between us, but I am still your father. Show me some respect son!!"

"Why should I? You didn't show mom any respect. If it wasn't for Tameeka showing me how to love and respect a woman, I would be a loose cannon."

"I think everyone needs to calm down and take a breather," Meeka handed Isabella to Sydney and jumped to her feet. She stood in the middle of the living room with her hands extended out. She wasn't going to tolerate any shouting or disrespect in her home.

"Brink, your father is checking into a rehab facility this Friday. He's finally getting the help we wanted him to get." Tori said as she smiled and grabbed Brink Senior's hand. Hustle stared at their locked hands and rolled his eyes.

"No mom, THAT'S THE HELP YOU ALWAYS WANTED! YOU'VE BEEN HOLDING ONTO THAT BECAUSE ONE DAY YOU WANTED TO BE WITH DAD AGAIN! What if he relapses and leaves you in the wind again? Who's going to pick up the pieces of your shattered heart? It's going to be Brink Junior and not Brink Senior as usual. Mom, aren't you tired of dad tampering with your heart? Dad, aren't you tired of tampering with mom's heart? I'm sick of this shit. Tameeka let them out when they are ready."

"It's not a crime to give your dad another chance," Tori shouted.

"Can yall not shout in my house? Our daughter is sitting right here." Meeka said.

"I'll take Isabella to her room," Sydney whispered and walked out of the living room. A few seconds later she reentered the living room and quietly took her seat next to Hustle.

"Mom, in this situation, it's a fucking crime to take him back. I should have your crazy ass arrested now. Too bad the cops hate Meeka and I, and they won't come to our house!"

"Brink!" Meeka shouted, but Hustle ignored her.

"No Tameeka, let him go. When things get tough, he runs. That's what he did as a kid, and I can see nothing ass changed." Brink Senior said.

"What about your dad, what do you do? Seems like when things got tough with you, you picked up a random hoe, a drug house, or a pipe. Matter of fact, let him out right now. Mom, if you want to leave with him you can bounce as well," Hustle stood to his feet and opened the front door.

Then he stormed out of the living room and raced up the stairs. Everyone's eyes followed him, and they were startled when he slammed the bedroom door shut. Meeka covered her eyes and dropped her head. She understood that Brink was upset, but his immature ways embarrassed her.

"I'm sorry yall. Brink is under a lot of stress, and this right here is a lot for him to handle."

"That is no excuse for him to act in that manner! Brink is a grown man, and he needs to know how to control his actions!" Tori snapped.

"Yes, he is a grown man, but deep down inside he's still that little boy who needs his father in his life! You haven't seen one another in ten years, and you thought this visit was going to go smooth? You came into my home without permission and have the nerve to talk slick about Hustle."

"Who the heck is Hustle?" Brink Senior asked and laughed.

"Hustle is Brink's nickname, but of course you don't know that. I think this is enough mingling for the day.

Mrs. Tori and Mr. Brink, you two have a good day," Meeka walked to the door and stood next to it. With an attitude, Tori grabbed her purse and walked out of the house. Brink Senior grabbed his black trench coat and did the same. Meeka closed the door and squatted to the ground. She buried her face in her lap and screamed in a low tone.

"Meeka, are you good?" Sydney asked

"Yea Sydney I'm good, but more and more I realize that Hustle's family is fucked up. I thought I was the one with the fucked up family? Let me run upstairs and check on him," Meeka ran upstairs and walked down the hall quietly. She peeked into Isabella's room and found her lying across her bed with her soft pink blanket in her hand. Meeka smiled at the innocent sight and whispered, "I wish you could stay like this forever," Meeka blew kisses at Isabella and walked away. She slowly walked into her bedroom and found Hustle standing on the balcony. She could hear him sniffing, and it put a damper on her heart. It wasn't often that she heard or witness Hustle crying, but when she did, it saddens her.

"Hey, come here," Meeka whispered. Hustle turned around, but he didn't move. Instead, Meeka sped walked to the balcony and stood in front of Hustle. "Hey, it's okay baby. I love you, and I'm here for you," Meeka softly grabbed Brink by his cheek and kissed his lips. Without replying, he smiled and placed his head on her shoulder.

"Make sure them muthafuckas are out of my house. I had enough of my mom for the month."

***

The day that no one thought would come, especially Meeka. Everyone thought Meeka would face jail time because of pimping, but that wasn't the case. Four days ago, she was booked and charged with simple battery, disturbing the peace, aggravated assault, and a convicted felon possession of a firearm charge. Meeka spotted Jason at a gas station on the east side of Opelousas and everything she promised Sydney escaped her mind. One thing lead to another, and things got crazy. He pulled a gun out on Meeka, but that didn't scare her. The sight of his hands shaking while clutching the trigger made her laugh. Jason was so afraid, he dropped the gun, and they began to fight for it. Not only was Jason's fingerprints on the gun so was Meeka's. Meeka pleaded guilty to all the charges except one, possession of a firearm. With the little power that Austin has, he was able to charge Meeka with the gun and Jason was only charged with disturbing the peace. Meeka was furious and knew Austin tampered with the evidence. She didn't have physical evidence, but she knew he was behind it.

"What time is it?" Meeka asked Sydney.

Meeka held the phone against her ear and listened to Sydney cry on the phone. She rubbed her dry face and eyes. Every time she called Sydney, she would cry, and Meeka hated. She thought about to not calling her, but she that would make matters worse.

"It's 4:15 pm Meek, do you need the date also?" Sydney reached for her box of tissue and pulled a few out. Then she blew her nose loudly, and Meeka pulled her ear away from the phone. The sight of the heavy snot disgusted her, and she was tempted to disconnect the call.

"No, it's Saturday right, the 16th?" Meeka asked.

"Yea, it is, a cold front came today. You know when the wind blows everyone runs to put their winter gear on." Sydney laughed and wiped her tears.

"That's my city for you, but tomorrow they're going to be in shorts and tank tops." Meeka laughed.

"You got that right, that's how it usually goes. How are you though Meek?"

"I'm good Syd. I got a visit today."

"What, from who was it Brink?" Sydney asked.

"That's funny I wish it was from him."

"Well, who was it from?!"

"Your husband paid me a visit today just to laugh in my face. This is the day he's been waiting for, but I won't be here for long." She laughed.

"I can't stand Austin with every bone in my damn body! He's only trying to kick you while you're down, but don't let him get to you Meeka! On a better note, in four months he will no longer be my husband. Thank you for that blessing God, Mary, and Jesus!" Sydney said as she cleared her throat.

"Trust me I won't. Marlo has a cake baked for him, don't worry."

"Oh for real, I'm guessing you spoke to your lawyer," Meeka asked.

"Yes I did, yesterday actually and I nearly picked her up when she gave me the good news." Sydney laughed.

"That's good Syd, that's good news, by then everything will be back to normal. I'm not sure how the business is going to work out with that, but either way, you'll be divorced or a widow." Meeka laughed and looked over her shoulders. Even though the phone call was being recorded, she still wanted to make sure no one was close by listening to her conversation. If an officer overheard her talking in code about killing a detective, her jail time could change for the worse.

"At this point Meek, I don't care at ALL! As long as I'm back to my maiden name and no longer attached to him, I'm good."

"I feel you on that, but guess who I spoke to earlier?" Meeka asked.

"Who?" Sydney asked.

"I spoke to Tori, and she told me Brink Senior is still in rehab. By the look of things, he's doing good, and they are back together."

"Wow, I guess true love doesn't die," Sydney shrugged her shoulders and stood to her feet. She walked into the kitchen and inhaled the tasteful smell. Xavier stood at the stove with a pink apron wrapped around his lower half and a long metal spoon in his hand. In the clockwise motion, he stirred a big pot of seafood gumbo. Sydney couldn't wait dive into the pot and enjoy that gumbo.

She walked behind Xavier and stood on her tiptoes. He slightly looked over his shoulder and kissed her lips. Sydney smiled and kissed him back. She and Xavier are back together and in a great space in their relationship. Besides the information the news article provided, Xavier wasn't up to date on why Meeka was in jail. Sydney liked it that way and planned to keep it that way, the less who knew, the better. When Jason was asked what happened between him and Meeka, he didn't tell the truth behind the argument. Even though Meeka hated Jason, she liked him for lying. That kept everyone out of their business.

"I guess so, but in my case…I'm not so sure. I don't know what's going on with Brink and me."

"Has his mom tried to talk to him?" Sydney asked.

"Yes, and she said he flashed out on her. I fucked up bad Syd, and he's taking it out on everyone," Meeka exhaled and pressed the phone against her chest. Tears filled her eyes, but she wiped them away. She could hear Sydney speaking to her, but she couldn't make out the words. More tears formed in her eyes, but she used her sleeves to wipe them away.

"Did you do what I asked you Sydney?" Meeka asked.

"Yea I went by your house, but he told me the same thing he told you."

"What to leave him alone?" Meeka asked.

"I'm sorry Meeka. Yes, that's what he said. I know he's still upset, but he'll eventually stop acting like a fool. You know Hustle can't stay mad at you for long. I'll try again later when I pick up the boys from the Boys and Girls club." Sydney said.

"Okay, Syd and thank you. How is the packing coming along?"

"Ugh, let's not talk about that. Pacson thinks the boxes are to make a clubhouse with! I have shit everywhere I swear Meek I can't wait until all this is over." As Sydney walked out of the kitchen, she dropped her shoulders and tossed her head backward. She kicked a few boxes down the hall and walked into her bedroom. Clothes, hangers, boxes, and shoes were everywhere. Sydney pushed the stack of clothes off the bed and laid across it. The clothes were neatly folded, and later she would regret tossing the clothes to the floor.

"Damn, that's the reason I don't move often. I'll fuck around and leave everything in the house. The new homeowners would have Christmas in July." Meeka laughed.

"You're crazy girl, and I'm glad that you still have your sense of humor."

"They take everything else when you come here, but that's the one thing they can't take," Meeka said.

"Meek, as soon as you get out, I want yall to come to Atlanta. You're going to need a vacation when you get out of jail."

"I will Sydney, and that's my word. I can't promise you that it will be a yall, but it will definitely be me. First Pedro, then Forty, and now you! It seems like everyone is moving forward and I'm standing still."

"It doesn't have to be like that when you get home Meeka. I'm ready for a fresh start, and so was Pedro and Forty. A fresh start would do you wonderful, I know it will."

"It's easier said than done Sydney, but we'll talk about that later. It's a minute left on the call, and I don't want it to end while we're talking." Meeka said.

"Okay Meeka, call me later, I love you."

"I love you too and kiss the boys for me." Meeka smiled and said.

"I will, bye."

"Bye Syd," Meeka slowly pulled the phone from her ear and placed it back on the receiver. As she walked to the cell, the only thing she could think about was Hustle and how he was acting cold towards her. Since she was arrested, she has only spoken to him twice. He was so pissed and disappointment that Meeka put herself in this situation, he couldn't tolerate talking to her. Meeka couldn't handle not hearing Hustle's voice, but she didn't have any other option. Every time she called him, she could only speak to Isabella. Once the conversation was done, he ended the calls without speaking to her or saying goodbye.

She walked to her cell and spotted a new cellmate sitting on the edge of the bed. Her long blonde her covered her face, her head hung low, and she seemed nervous. Meeka nodded her head at Blondie to grab her attention and pointed at the girl. Blondie stood to her feet and said, "Sarah, this is Tameeka, Meeka this is Sarah."

"What's up Sarah?" Meeka nodded her head and walked to her bunk. Sarah's belongings sat next to her, so Meeka grabbed them and placed them on the top bunk.

"I – am – am at the top bunk?" She asked.

"Yep, you are, is that a problem?" Meeka sized Sarah up and down waiting for her to reply. She quickly climbed to the top of the bunk and said, "No, it's not." Sarah presented herself like a fragile white girl who basically was a pushover. Meeka knew she would have to take Sarah under her wing until she was released.

"Meek, you have that girl shaken like a stripper. You better tell her to get it together or them dykes will get a hold of her," Blondie clapped her hands and laughed. Sarah's eyes grew big, and she turned to Meeka. She started to cry, but Meeka grabbed her hand and said, "Sarah, it's too early for that crying shit. Blondie is only joking with you. What are you in here for?"

"I got caught stealing." She mumbled.

"Stealing what?" Meeka and Blondie asked.

"I hope a car or something big with the way you're crying," Meeka chuckled and shook her bed. Then she rubbed her nose and leaned against the bed.

"No, I was stealing a pack of underwear." Blondie laughed, but Meeka didn't. It was more to Sarah's story, and she wanted to find out why she tried to steal the underwear.

"Girl, you're crying because of that? You won't be here for long, I'm sure your family will have you out by tomorrow." Blondie said.

"How old are you?" Meeka asked.

"I'm eighteen, and I don't know how long I'm going to be in here. My parents don't have money to bond me out nor do they have money to buy me underwear, and I needed some badly."

"Do you always steal or was that your first time?" Meeka asked.

"I always steal, but this was the first time I got caught. Three months ago, I got into a fight on the job, and they fired him. My mom gets a social security check, but that barely pays the bills. By next month we'll be behind on the rent and on the verge of getting evicted."

"Damn, I'm sorry to hear that. All I can tell you is keep your head up lil' one, it can't rain forever," Blondie yawned and rolled over. Meeka signaled for Sarah to come down and she did. She sat next to Meeka with her arms wrapped around her body and her legs crossed tightly.

"If I get out before you, I'll bond you out. If this is your first time being booked, your bond will be a couple of hundred dollars." Meeka smiled.

"Wow, you would do something like that for someone you don't know?" Sarah asked.

"Yes, I would," Meeka said.

If you don't mind me asking, why would you do that? Do I have to pay you back when I get out because I can't? I couldn't even send my college application off because I didn't have the money."

"Sarah, you don't have to pay me back. My bank account will not notice that change is gone."

"What do you do?" Sarah asked.

"I get money for a living, that's what I do. Since things are hard at home, why haven't you gotten a job? I know a lot of people hate working for $7.25 or fast food, but why haven't you gotten a job?" Meeka asked.

"I was working at Wendy's, but my mom's car broke down last month. We live in Cresview Apartments and walking to work was killing me. In the past month, I've walked in every kind of weather."

"Damn, if I get you a car, will you go back to work and maintain it?" Meeka asked.

"Hell yea I would, but why would you do any of this for me?" Sarah asked.

"I'm doing this because you remind me of myself. It takes a real go-getter to steal a pack of underwear. I see someone that needs help, and I will help them. You have to keep your promise, you hear me?"

"Yes ma'am I do, thank you so much." Sarah wrapped her arms around Meeka and gave her a hug. Meeka didn't know Sarah, but the hug meant a lot to her.

***

Meeka was anxious, but nervous as she waited for Hustle and Isabella to arrive. She hated that her daughter had to see her in an orange jumpsuit and behind a dirty glass. She missed her so much, she couldn't take it anymore. Her every thought was about Hustle and Isabella, and it was driving her crazy. She constantly thought about all the times they shared together and regretted that she didn't cherish them.

Meeka sat on the rusty stool and stretched her neck to see all the visitors walk in. Some people waved, and some whispered at the sight of Meeka in jail. The person who was once covered in diamonds, expensive weave, and fur coats was now dressed in orange with a sleek ponytail.

"Damn girl, you look nervous," Cookie scratched her itchy scalp and sat next to Meeka. She nodded her head and said, "Hell yea I am, I miss them so much."

"Girl the way he talks to you on the phone, I wouldn't be surprised if he didn't miss you." She chuckled.

"Don't get me wrong, he misses me. I can hear it in his voice he misses me a lot, but he's angry. I don't blame him at all. I would have an attitude as well."

"I guess girl, whatever you say." Cookie said.

Meeka was a little embarrassed, so she covered her face. She felt like she was an animal at the zoo and everyone wanted to pet her. Meeka was the talk of the town, and everyone was shocked that she was in prison.

"There goes my boo," Cookie jumped to her feet and waved at the heavy set woman that walked her way. Meeka laughed to herself. She was shocked that this was the person Cookie always spoke about. She forgot to mention her boo was a woman who looked like she recently was released from prison.

Meeka caught Hustle's attention and waved him her way. He didn't show any emotion as he walked in her direction. He sat on a stool with Isabella on his lap. Meeka nearly jumped out of her skin because she was excited.

"Izzy!" Meeka squealed and smiled. Isabella smiled and reached for the glass.

"Mommy!" She said.

"Yes baby, it's mommy. Oohhh I miss you so much." Meeka began to cry, but she wiped her tears. Hustle shook his head and exhaled.

"Don't cry now, you should have listened to me." Hustle rolled his eyes and shook his head again.

"I know, and I told you I was sorry. I should have listened to you from day one. Now I'm in this dump until my lawyer gets me out." She said.

"Yea you should have listened to me. Speaking of your lawyer, I spoke to her today." Hustle said.

"Really, what did Taneisha say? She better had said something good with all the money she makes from me."

"By the looks of things, she'll have you out of here by next Tuesday." Hustle said.

"What, are you serious?" Meeka reached to grab Hustle's hand, but she was reminded of the glass that separated them. The guard gave her a stale look, and she calmed down.

"Yea, but we'll be gone by then." Hustle said.

"What are you talking about and who is we?" Meeka asked.

"We as in Isabella and myself, I told you I wasn't going to do this."

"Brink....don't do this, especially now. I need you to be here for me, why would you not be here for me?" Meeka's lips trembled and her eyes watered with tears. She glanced at Isabella and dropped her head.

"Tameeka I gave you all the time in the world to get it together. I gave you MORE than enough time to get it together, and everyone knows that. I can't do this shit anymore!"

"Baby please, I'm literally begging you. DO NOT LEAVE ME! I'm nothing without you and Isabella. Look at me I'm not myself at all. I'm stressing, losing weight already, and my hair is falling out! I miss you two, and it's killing me!! Just imagine how I would be without you two!"

"I DON'T CARE ABOUT THAT TAMEEKA!! Time after time I've watch you do shit I wouldn't do. I'm a man, and I wouldn't do half the shit you do. I'm not living this life with you anymore. If you want to live this lifestyle, find you a new nigga." Hustle said.

"I don't want a new nigga. I just need time to get my head straight." Meeka mumbled.

"Didn't I give you a fair warning and a deadline?"

"Yes, you did bu…"

"Okay, and did you meet that deadline?" He interrupted.

"No, I didn't, bu…"

"My point eexxaacccttttllllyyy, that is it! You know I love you with all my heart, but I have to do what's best for us."

"But you bring out the best in ME Brink, don't you see that?" Meeka cried.

"No, I don't see it." Hustle said.

"Yes, you do see it! How could you not see it?"

"Because if I brought the best out in you, none of this would have happened. We're moving to San Diego, California like I said. I found a nice daycare to enroll her in. The neighborhood is great, way better than this shit ass city. I'm going to hire a nanny to help me until I get into the groove of things." Hustle said.

"You have all this figured out, I can't believe you. How can you do this to me, how? How can you do this to our family?"

"You need to ask yourself those questions. I'm cleaning up the mess that you made. HOW COULD YOU DO THIS TO OUR FAMILY? You know I love you, that's why you do the shit you do. I want to marry you and be with you for the rest of my life, but not like this. If you love me like you say you do, you would have never put me through all this bullshit! I'm sorry I'm being so harsh, but I can't think about your feelings right now. My only concern is Isabella and what's best for her."

"So taking her across the country is 'what's best for her'? Wait a minute, is there another woman? Man, it has to be another woman who has you tripping like this." Meeka became furious, but Hustle chuckled.

"Wow, why can't you accept the fact that this is your fault? You're the issue and not anyone else. Moving to San Diego isn't a permanent move, but it's a step to a fresh start. I won't keep you away from her that would be cruel on my part. What I am keeping her away from is the bullshit. I pray to God that you don't become number one on that list. You need to focus on getting out of here first and getting your shit together. Then you can come and visit us, but you can't take her back home with you." Hustle said.

"Brink, she's my daughter, I carried her for nine months. I'm together I'm all the way together. Nothing you're saying is making sense to me," Meeka clinched her fist tightly, and her lips stretched wide. Hustle was pissing her off, and the fact that she couldn't hit him pissed her off more.

"Tameeka, look me in my eyes right now. Can you tell me that you're done with the game? Meeka stared Hustle in the eyes, but she didn't reply. Hustle titled his head and said, "Cool, cool, not even for your daughter. I never thought I would call you this, but you're an unfit mother. Yea I said it, now get mad. You can't do much behind a glass, but get upset!"

"Excuse me, what makes you better than me? You were right next to me doing the crazy shit I was doing. Let's be honest, half the time you didn't try and stop me. Did you think about the consequences we could have faced? NO, so that makes you unfit as well. Get the fuck out of here with that weak shit because I'm not buying it."

"Call it what you want, but unlike you, I caught my head. Yea I let you do some crazy shit because once again, I love you. I know if you snap your fingers for a new man, a line of guys would be waiting for you. You want the truth, and that's the truth. I don't know what more you want from me Tameeka. You think when I first met you I saw any of this in our future? I thought I would be on the other side of that glass and not you. I really don't understand what more you want from me. I gave you everything baby, I swear I did."

"You don't think I did the same in return? You don't see I'm crazy over you? I want you and only you, it's been that way. No one can compare to you Brink, you're my best friend. If you feel like this is what's best for her, do what you have to do. Just make sure it's the best decision for HER and not anyone else. Goodbye Isabella, mommy loves you," Meeka took one look at Isabella and kissed the glass. She hated to leave Isabella, but she didn't have any other options.

Meeka fought back her tears as much as possible, and so did Hustle. Neither one of them knew what to say. He pressed his open hand against the glass and said, "I love you Tameeka." His emotional and cracked voice made her weak.

"HUSTLE WAIT, I PROMISE I WILL CHANGE!! I PROMISE I WILL CHANGE! BUT DON'T LEAVE ME HERE! I can't live without you and my baby." Hustle stopped, but he continued walking. Meeka screamed his name again, and he stopped again. The tears streamed down his face, and he turned around so Meeka could see them. His mind told him to continue walking, but his heart told him something different. When it came to Meeka that was the only love he knew. He couldn't give up just yet.

"Are you moving with us?" He asked.

"Yes, I am, I love you."

"I love you too. Now relax while I get you out of here."

Chapter 5

Meeka felt like a run away slave once she walked out of jail after three weeks. She kept her promise and bailed Sarah out of jail and purchased her a car. She promised to keep in touch with her and Meeka meant that. She couldn't stop talking about Sarah to Hustle and how much Sarah reminded her of herself. Marlo kept his promise and handled Austin. The way Marlo disposed of his body no one would ever find a trace of DNA. Meeka felt the weight of the world lifting off her shoulders and could now be comfortable once she left Louisiana.

Meeka arrived at Roman's home, but she noticed a car parked next to his. She wasn't sure whose it was, but she didn't care. Meeka needed to let Roman know she was out of jail and to tell him goodbye. She adjusted her rearview mirror and checked her lipstick and nose. Her pink lipstick was still smooth, and her nose was booger free. Once she was done, she grabbed her wallet off the seat and slid it under the driver's sit. Meeka was a little nervous for some reason, but she shook the feeling off. It was only Roman, and it wasn't her first time visiting him.

She adjusted the mirror again and took one more look at herself and smiled. She could honestly admit to herself that she felt like a different woman. She felt like the woman everyone knew she was destined to be.

Meeka stepped out of the car and closed the door. As she walked to the front door, she fumbled with her fingers to keep calm. The front door opened and Roman had his arm around a woman's slim hips. He kissed her on her thin lips, and she smiled. Then she wrapped her arms around his neck and gave Roman another kiss. Meeka was a little shocked, but she couldn't deny that the woman was stunning. Her dark chocolate skin seemed smooth and wrinkle free, and her bone straight onyx black hair looked luscious, thick, and healthy. Her dark brown eyes complimented her long lashes well.

Roman stared at the woman and love overflowed in his eyes. Meeka exhaled and smiled to herself. She knew that look because she was used to the reason he looked like that. Therefore, the woman had to be someone special to him.

"I'll call you when I get to the airport baby, I love you," she said.

"Okay, I love you too, drive carefully." Roman kissed her on the cheek then turned to the door. He was a little surprised to see Meeka standing in his yard, but he played it cool.

"Tameeka, what's up?" He waved and smiled. Before greeting Roman, she walked to the woman and extended her hand out. They shook hands and smiled at one another.

"Hi, I'm Tameeka."

"Hello, I'm Jesse. It's nice to meet you." She said.

"Jesse, this is my friend Tameeka," Roman said.

"Oh okay, well it's nice to meet you again Tameeka. I have to go, baby, seriously." Jesse said.

"Alright, be careful."

"I will," Jesse gave Roman a hug and smiled at Meeka. Meeka cracked a smile and gave a small wave.

Once Jesse got into her car and drove off, Roman and Meeka entered his house. Meeka looked around and noticed a few things were different since the last time she was there. Jesse had to be the reason for the silk curtains and fake plants in the living room.

"I like what you have done with the place," Meeka said.

"Thank Jesse for the redecorating. I can't take the credit for it." He chuckled and led Meeka into the living room. She dropped her keys on the couch and sat down a few inches away from Roman. The home was comfortable and such a familiar place, she didn't want to leave.

"I guess Roman," Meeka rolled her eyes and flipped her hair in a sarcastic way. Roman grabbed her hand and laughed.

"You are the last person I expected to see today," Roman said.

"I could see it all in your face when we locked eyes."

"Jesse played it cool, but she's going to ask me a million questions." He shook his head and laughed. Meeka shrugged her shoulders and crossed her legs. Roman stared at every inch of Meeka's body in her skin tight dress. She purposely wore royal blue because it was Roman's favorite color. He exhaled and rubbed his hands on his thighs. The way Meeka looked in that dress, he was ready to risk it all with no regrets.

"Jesse must be something special to you?"

"That's my girlfriend, are you jealous?" He joked.

"You know I am, you're forever my baby." Meeka laughed.

"Awww, shit like that makes me want to be single forever."

"I wish I could have the best of both worlds." She implied and smiled.

"I bet you do. What's up though, you're looking good for someone who just got out of prison." He laughed.

"Kiss my ass, Ro. I was in in the parish jail. I wasn't in San Quentin State Prison." Meeka rolled her eyes and gently pushed his chest.

"You know I'm joking, but when did you get out?" He asked.

"I actually got out a few hours ago. I wanted to stop by and tell you thank you for your encouraging letter. It really helped me keep my head together."

"You know it's all good. I damn near lost my mind when I heard it was you tearing it down at the gas station. That's crazy how they tried to pin that gun on you, dirty ass cops."

"I know, but I can't dwell on the past. I'm just happy that I'm free and I won't ever see that place again. I missed Brink and Isabella so much when I was in there," Meeka shook her head and stared at the ground.

"I bet you did miss them. So, this was your first stop? I can't believe daddy wasn't waiting for you with open arms." He laughed.

"This was my first stop actually, so you're right. I wanted to thank you for the encouraging words you sent me. Your letter meant a lot to me, and I will keep it forever."

"You're welcome, but if this was your first stop, where is your man?"

"He's away right now. Marlo was there to pick me up."

"Hustle should have been there. I would break up with him." He laughed.

"I bet you would want me to move on." She grinned, and so did Roman.

"Of course I would, and you would be back here, but I know where your heart is. If your heart wasn't with Hustle, I would have her shit packed and at the door." He joked.

"Oh, so that means she's living here? Wow, you're moving fast, that's a first time."

"Not quite, but she does have a few basic things here. I like her, but I want to take things slow with her." He said.

"Okay, I feel you on that. She seems like a nice girl, and she's beautiful." Meeka said.

"She is, but she isn't you. It's something about your smile and laughter that will always drive me crazy. You know my mom always asks about you."

"I've been meaning to visit her, but things have been crazy. Tell her I said hello and I'll drop by tomorrow. I would hate to leave without seeing her." Meeka said.

"You're leaving, where are you going?" Roman asked.

"I am moving to San Diego. Hustle and Isabella left a few days ago. I would be a fool to let my family fall apart like this. Despite the things I have done to Hustle, that is where my heart lies."

"I respect you on that, and I hope everything works out."

"Thanks, Ro." She smiled.

"No problem. When are you leaving?" He asked.

"I'm aiming for this week, but I'm not sure. Marlo contacted a realtor while I was in jail and our houses are on the market. There is a couple from Harvey, Louisiana who is interested in buying one of my houses. The other house hasn't gotten any offers yet. Until Marlo leaves, he'll stay in that house."

"You're really serious about this move?" He asked.

"Yes, I am, why wouldn't I be? Nothing is here for me, and I have to make this right. Hustle won't wait around forever."

"You're right about that, he isn't me. I'll wait around forever for you." His charming smile made Meeka blush. She bit her bottom lip and shook her head.

"Stop it Roman, your slick ass always had a way with words." She giggled.

"That's because I learned from the best. I've seen you talk your way out of plenty of situations."

"You are right about that, I'm a smooth operator. On a serious note, would you wait forever for me?" She asked.

"Of course Tameeka, I'm waiting now." He laughed.

"Wow, that's crazy. You are a great guy Roman."

"Jesse is cool, and we've been dating for two months now. She's a manager at the Hilton Inn Hotel in Lafayette."

"Oh, okay, is she from Lafayette as well?" Meeka asked.

"Naw, she's from Scott," Roman said.

"Are things serious between you two?"

"You can say that. You know I don't play about relationships. Things are going good between us. I hope it stays this way."

"It sounds like someone is in llloooooooovvvvvvvvvveeeeeee." Meeka laughed and tilted her head in the air. Roman squinted his eyes at her and shrugged his shoulders.

"I can definitely say I'm falling in love with her." He smiled.

"That's good Ro, you deserve someone that makes you happy. She does make you happy, right?"

"Yes Tameeka, she does."

"Well that's good, everyone deserves happiness. If she breaks your heart, I'm going to beat her ass. I will literally catch the first flight to Louisiana and beat her ass." She laughed.

"I'll keep that in mind, but you better pray. Brink opens the door when you get there."

"It's funny, but it's true. Brink can be harsh at times. I hope he doesn't change his mind when I get there." She rolled her eyes.

"Honestly Meek, can you blame him?" Roman asked.

"I can't blame him. I've done some messed up things to him. At least I know it's time to make it right. I'm getting too old and tired for this shit."

"You'll never be too old or tired. It's just time to leave the game alone. Leave that headache for them, young kids. Focus on your health, your family, and investing your money in a few things."

"Thanks, Ro, I appreciate it." She smiled.

"Besides all of that, how are you? You've had a lot happen in a short period of time. I would have lost my mind if I lost both of my best friends. I know Juju was like a sister to you, well, Santana too." He laughed. Meeka's smile slowly faded away and she thought about the horrible night her mind played tricks on her. She needed to tell Roman the truth about Justice. He was a solid guy, so she wasn't worried about him telling anyone she killed Justice.

"I'm going to always be hurt about Santana's death. Santana was like my other boyfriend, you know." Meeka laughed.

"Santana was good people. It's sad he had to go out like that. Whoever killed Justice had to be a straight sava..."

"Before you finish that sentence, I need to tell you something," Meeka demanded. She sat on her hands and rock side to side. She wasn't sure how to tell Roman the truth. She knew it was wrong to cut him off in midsentence, but she couldn't let him finish speaking. There was no way she could sit there and let him say another word about her.

"Tell me what Meek?" He asked.

"I'm..." Meeka stopped speaking and covered her mouth. She cleared her throat then said, "I'm the savage who killed Justice."

"What, are you for real?" Roman asked.

"Yea, that bitch betrayed me in a way I never thought she would."

"Did you kill Miami as well?" He asked.

"No, my young boys did that. She wasn't worth getting my hands dirty. Justice, on the other hand, I had to do it myself. That shit was beyond personal, and I don't feel bad for killing her. She called Sydney to meet up on Cosay Road to 'talk.' Justice had a wire on, just how her brother told her to do in the recording. She tried to make Sydney work against me, and if she wouldn't, she was going to shoot her. She had the gun with a bullet in the chamber. I didn't want to do it Ro, but I had to. It didn't matter if I snitched or not, a lot of people would have come down with me. I expected everyone else to betray me, even Sydney, but not Juju. Justice was literally like family to me, but I guess that wasn't enough for her."

"You know they say water is thicker than blood." Roman implied.

"That's true, but in this situation, I'm not sure what side she is on. All of this is crazy Roman, and I'm not sure if I can handle it all."

"You did handle it all, but it's time for you to get away from here. I know that move to California is going to be great for you. Don't come back, stay away." He laughed.

"I'm going to miss you though Ro." She laughed and pretended to pout. Roman laughed and leaned closer to Meeka. He kissed her forehead and rubbed her thigh. Meeka placed her soft hand on his cheek and kissed his lips. It was a friendly kiss, but she liked the affection they showed one another.

"You never know, I might show up in your city unannounced one day."

"That would nice, I wouldn't mind seeing a familiar face. Especially a handsome, familiar face, you are something, serious baby." Meeka laughed and softly squeezed Roman's left bicep. He laughed a little and began to flex.

"I try to be a little something. I still can't believe you were in jail though. Not pretty lil' Meeka in a dirty cell." He laughed and clapped his hands.

"I'm built for a lot of things, but jail isn't one of them. That muthafucka Parish Jail is terrible and needs to shut down." She laughed.

"Trust me I know. I had my time there twice. Never will any jail see me. It's not my Safe Haven." Meeka wanted to continue the conversation, but her phone began to ring. She glanced at the screen, and it was Hustle returning her phone call. Meeka hit the silent button and said, "I have to go. I'm dying to talk to my daughter, and I don't know what kind of mood Brink is in. It was nice seeing you, Roman. I'm going to miss you."

"You know the pleasure is all mines. It was nice seeing you as well."

"I bet, take care of yourself handsome." Meeka smiled and planted a kiss on Roman's cheek. A single tear dropped from her left eye, but she wiped it away. This was another part of her past she had to leave behind.

***

"I swear, Meek, Georgia is nice and all, but this traffic!! I'm from the country, and I am NOT use of this," Sydney gently banged her head against the steering wheel and groaned. It was 4:30 pm, but she's been stuck in traffic since 3:00 pm. Every day she called Meeka complaining about traffic and Meeka laughed.

"You should have stayed your ass here where it's no traffic. You can breeze through the city with no problem."

"Very funny, Meeka, I see you became a comedian overnight." Sydney joked.

"Yep and my first show is tonight staring you. You know your country ass don't belong in the big city." Meeka laughed.

"Whatever, but when are yall coming to visit? I miss you already, and the boys are asking about you and Isabella."

"We miss you guys also, but I have to fly to California first. Once we get settled there, we'll fly to Atlanta, that's my word."

"Damn it, I have to go, Xavier is calling me."

"Okay, bye, Syd." Meeka scrolled through the frozen treats aisle at the grocery store trying to figure out what she wanted for dessert. One second she wanted ice cream, but the next second she wanted a delicious frozen pie. Every second she stared at the cart hoping and praying that Isabella would be in there. She missed her daughter's laughter and the way she begged for every treat she laid her eyes on. Meeka could never tell Isabella no, and she always got her way. Every time they came home with a car full of treats, Hustle went crazy. Meeka didn't care, she always laughed it off. In her eyes, Isabella was a princess, and she deserved everything she got.

"Hey, Meeka, I'm glad to see you're out." A random girl with a head full of box braids waved at Meeka as she walked by. Meeka gave her a fake smile and waved back. She wasn't sure who the girl was or if it was another setup. If it was, she was going to be smarter this time. Meeka grabbed her purse and tucked it tightly under her arm.

Walmart was packed and full of loud and rowdy people. All of the noise made Meeka uncomfortable, and she was ready to leave the store.

"Girl yea, I'm going to Roman's house when I leave here." Hearing Roman's name made Tameeka's heart skip a beat. The voice was one she only heard once before. She wasn't sure if it's who she thought it was, but Meeka wasn't trying to find out. She carefully looked over her shoulder and spotted Jesse at the end of the aisle. While Meeka was wearing sweatpants and an oversized hoodie, Jesse looked like she just stepped out of a Vogue magazine.

Her hair was wand hair and highlighted cherry red. Her red floor length maxi dress fitted her perfectly, and her round booty poked out. Her waist was snatched, but her hips flared out just right. Meeka didn't want to stare too much because she didn't want to get caught, but she couldn't help it. She didn't know what her mind frame was, but Jesse was a bad bitch. If she examined her from head to toe, it would be impossible to spot a flaw.

Not many women could make Tameeka feel insecure, but Jesse did. Everything about her seems perfect, and Meeka was far from perfect. She tried to stare at Jesse a little longer, but Jesse noticed someone staring at her.

"Shit," Meeka whispered.

"Samantha, let me call you when I get to Roman's house, bye," Jesse disconnected the call and dropped her iPhone into her purse. Meeka continued to stare at the Blue Bell Ice cream as if Jesse wasn't in her presence. In the corner of her left eye, she could see the smirk of Jesse's face as she approached her.

"Well, well, well, hello Miss Money Making Meeka."

"Only people that know me call me that. It's Tameeka to you." Meeka snapped.

"Okay, Miss Tameeka, whatever you like. How are you doing on this fine evening?" Jesse licked her lips and tilted her head to the left. Her arms were tight across her chest, and she tapped her foot on the floor. By her body language and firm voice, Meeka knew Jesse wanted to get something off her chest.

"Hello, Jessica, that is your name, right," Meeka shook her head and chuckled.

"It's Jesse, but I guess you don't remember that."

"Am I supposed to remember your name? We only met once, and I was sure that would be the last time. I guess I was wrong again, but what's up? You seem a little....TENSE baby girl. Your lips are tight, sweat is forming on your forehead, and that neck vein is throbbing like a pussy that hasn't been touched in months," Meeka stretched her hand out to touch the vein, but Jesse backed away. Meeka laughed and rolled her eyes.

"Don't touch me!" She snapped.

"Like I said, you seem tense. Is there something I need to know about Ro? Is he dead, in jail, the hospital, or did he vanish off the face off the earth?"

"His name is ROMAN, and I would like it if you kept my man's name out of your mouth."

"Your man, girl bye, before it was you, it was me. Let me put something in your ear really quick. RO was aaallllll about me. Everything RO did was based around me, you got that? We go way back, and we'll always be tight. I'm not sure what the hell your problem is, but I highly advise you fall the fuck back." Meeka said.

"Yea, that's right, he's my man and not yours. Trust me Tameeka, I know all about you and Roman. Don't think you two pulled one over my head that day. I know you still love him and he still loves you. Just about every day I catch him on your Instagram or Snapchat staring at your pictures. I don't know what you're telling him or trying to do, but you're the one who needs to fall back. Roman is the best thing that has happened to me, and I be damn if I let a chick like YOU come between us."

"A chick like me, Jessica, Jesse, or whatever your name is, you don't know shit about me. What Roman and I had is dead because I ended it. Believe me when I tell you this, if I wanted to bring it back to life, I could in a blink of an eye. It would be no problem at all sweetheart. He's a good man, but I'm happily taken. Like the man Ro is, he understood my decision to leave him and follow my heart. It doesn't matter who's in our lives, we will remain friends. You, Hustle, or anyone else that comes along can change that."

"Speaking of Hustle, didn't your man leave you while you were in jail? Maybe that's why you came to visit Roman. If you two thought yall played me, think again. I know all about you and disgust me!"

"I disgust you? Baby disgust is a strong word. In order to be disgusted by someone, you have to hate them. Since you only met me once, you shouldn't hate me." Meeka laughed.

"I don't have to know you to hate your type." She chuckled.

"There you go again with that shit. You're speaking as if you know me. Roman knows me, he knows me well actually. From the inside to the outside he knows me, top to bottom, and any other way you can think of. You, on the other hand, you know of me, and that's it. Please stop confusing the two, it's simple."

"I know enough about you to make a judgment, to not like your TYPE, and what you stand for."

"Let me guess, you heard about me in the streets, and you think you know? You heard I was a pimp, sold some drugs, and fucked a few bitches. That's like public information, therefore, you don't know me. You're just like the rest of these bitches who keep my name in their mouths. Yall as a whole should get tired of talking about me."

"I wonder how your daughter, Isabella, will feel when she finds out the truth about her mother. She's going to hate you just as much as the rest of the world does." Jesse laughed.

"Keep...my...daughter's name...out of your got damn mouth. I would hate to send you to Roman's house with a bloody mouth!"

"Try it if you want to. I'll scream and shout like a crazy woman. Then your ass will be back in the Parish Jail."

"Does Roman know he's dating a psychopath?" Meeka asked.

"I'm far from a psychopath, I'm the best thing that has happen to that man. You were the worst thing he has ever laid eyes on if you ask me. I heard how you hurt him, but I promise it won't happen again. Leave him alone and stay out of his life. He's happy, and he's good with me."

"Well thank God I'm not asking you. Actually, fuck your opinion and everything else. If I was a bad person, I would have cheated on him, but I didn't. Leaving Ro was the best decision for him and me. I'm with the person I want to be with and he can and will eventually find the person he is meant to be with. By the dumb shit that is coming out of your mouth, I doubt you're the one for him."

"You are so funny, it's pathetic." She laughed.

"What is your fake beef with me? Are you mad because I left him or are you mad because the man you love still loves me? Am I pimping one of your cousins or sibling's little girl? WHY ARE YOU SO DAMN MAD?" Meeka laughed.

"Little girl?"

"Yes, that's exactly what I said. You seem like a little girl who is mad she can't get any candy for supper. I know you bitches want to be like me, but damn, get over it."

"Girl, get over yourself fast. I'm going to say this again so you can get it through that weave of yours. I will not let you get in between Roman and I. That visit you made better be your last one. You have a good day Tameeka." Jesse gave Meeka a gracious stare and walked away. Meeka shook her head and silently laugh. In her mind, she pictured her nine-millimeter gun sending shots into Jesse's back. Lately, her mind was full of evil thoughts, and she couldn't control it. Jesse didn't bother looking back at Meeka as she walked away, but Meeka couldn't take her eyes off her. Jesse no longer intimidated her anymore. Jesse wasn't the woman Meeka thought she was. She was now a little girl. Meeka wanted to call Roman, but she changed her mind. She didn't want to cause any more confusion, but Jesse had her pissed to the max. She was so angry she started to laugh and shook it off.

Meeka opened the cooler and finally decided on what she wanted. She grabbed a quart of vanilla Blue Bell ice cream and dropped it into the cart. She thought about getting strawberry as well, but she changed her mind. She placed herself on a diet because she wanted to look good for Hustle.

"Meeka, Meeka, it's about time I ran into you," Meeka turned around and found Paulette Civil standing behind her with a huge smile.

Meeka smiled and said, "What up P, I've been trying to stay low key since I got out."

"Got out of what, please don't tell me jail?"

"Unfortunately, yes." Meeka sighed.

"Damn Meek, what happened, did that pimping shit go sour on you?"

"No, but it's a long story that I don't want to talk about," Meeka said.

"I understand that girl, but coming to Walmart wasn't a way to stay low key. I've seen at least two of your old boo's in here, including Stevie." Paulette laughed, but Meeka rolled her eyes.

"Oh Lord, I hope I don't run into her while in here or anywhere else."

"I don't blame you, Stevie hates your guts girl."

"I don't blame Steebie. I'm a piece of shit walking." Meeka said, and they both laughed.

"Girl don't say that about yourself," Paulette said.

"I'm just joking. When did you get back in town?" Meeka asked.

"I got back in town two days. I had to make a stop in Lake Charles first."

"Oh okay, that's what's up?" Meeka said.

"I'm sorry I couldn't make it to Santana or Juju's funeral. You know they had me deployed in Korea."

"I understand P, and it's all good."

Paulette Stevens was thirty-six-year-old from Lake Charles, Louisiana. She moved to Opelousas two years ago to be closer to family. Paulette was a good girl, but she still reminded Meeka of herself. Paulette was a go-getter and enlisting in the army was her come up.

"How are you doing by the way? I know you, Santana, and Justice were a tight click."

"I'm handling it one day at a time, that's the only thing I can do," Meeka shrugged her shoulders and nodded her head.

"I feel you on that, and I can only imagine your pain. I know it was hard losing both of your friends so close. I probably would have lost my mind and went crazy."

"I almost did, but I had to remember I have a lot to live for. What's done is done and losing my mind won't bring them back. The only thing I can do is keep their names alive." Meeka said.

"Is it true Sydney's husband is connected to Santana's death?" Paulette asked.

"That rumor was in the air, but he wasn't charged with anything. I guess people were just talking."

"I hope that was just a rumor and no one was stating facts. Sydney would be destroyed if it's true. How would you deal with your husband being tied to your friend's death?"

"They are actually in the middle of a divorce and hate one another," Meeka said.

"WHAT, ARE YOU FOR REAL, MEEKA?" Meeka shook her head, but Paulette couldn't believe what Meeka was saying. Everyone knew Austin and Sydney as the perfect couple. Some even compared their marriages to theirs and called them marriage goals.

"Yes, baby, Austin isn't the same person we know. He is a different person, a crazy person! He's even saying that I killed Juju, can you believe that?" Meeka said.

"Oh no, now Austin is tripping and losing HIS mind. I wouldn't believe that if Juju came from the dead and said it herself." She joked and laughed.

Meeka told Paulette this information because she knew Paulette would tell someone else. Then that person would tell another person, and everyone would know Austin was against Meeka. By the time the news would spread, Austin would be dead, and she would be out of Louisiana.

"I loved Juju more than Austin loved her, but I think he's trying to pin her death on anyone. Mainly someone that's connected to Sydney, which is crazy." Meeka said.

"Why is he trying to do that?" Meeka couldn't help but to notice how much Paulette moved while she spoke. She constantly rubbed her nose, and Meeka knew what that meant. She was waiting for Paulette to ask her and she was going to provide her with her fix.

"Sydney met a guy, and they fell in love rapidly. Their marriage was already rocky, and she filed for a divorce. The only thing I did was introduce Sydney to the guy because they were standing in each other's face. I didn't think they would fall in love that night." Meeka laughed.

"Well God damn. I guess love, at first sight, does exist." Paulette laughed.

"I know right, in Austin's eyes, I'm the reason for Sydney wanting the divorce. He said she's my *puppet*." Meeka rolled her eyes.

"Girl, bye, Sydney is grown and has a mind of her own," Paulette said.

"That's the same thing I've been shouting from day one," Meeka said.

"Say Meeka, do you have some girl on you? While I was in the Lake, I got a little something, but that was a little something. I need something for right now, and I'll hit you up later for some more."

"You know I got you and it's some good shit too." Meeka looked over her shoulders to make sure no one was watching her. Then she reached into her purse and shuffled around until she found a powder pack.

Paulette reached into her bag pocket and pulled out a small stack of money. She counted the money, then she handed Meeka a twenty dollar bill. Meeka held her hand tightly so she could make the transaction. Besides Meeka and Hustle, Paulette didn't purchase cocaine from anyone else in the city. She was embarrassed of her addiction and didn't want anyone else to know. No one in her family knew, including her boyfriend, and she planned to keep it that way. She wasn't embarrassed that Meeka and Hustle knew because she knew they wouldn't spread her business.

"Thanks, girl, I needed my fix badly. Do you have the same number? You know you change your number often?" She laughed.

"Yea, I do." She said.

Meeka didn't sell a lot of drugs, but she always kept a few powder packs on her just in case. Paulette looked like Miss Perfect on the outside, but on the inside was something different. Since the age of eighteen, Paulette has had an addiction to cocaine. She battled on and off to quit, but she could never stay clean. Meeka offered to check her into a rehab, but she declined the offer.

As Meeka and Paulette conversed, Jesse passed by with a mean mug on her face. Meeka laughed, but Paulette mugged her back and asked, "Meeka do we have a problem?"

"No problem at all, she's just mad." Meeka laughed.

"Damn Meek, she's still mad at that shit? If anyone should be mad, it's you."

"Wait, mad at what?"

"Girl that's Jesse from Sunset, you don't remember her?" Paulette asked.

"No, but am I supposed to remember her?" Meeka asked.

"Meeka you need to lay off that weed, that's Jesse, but her real name is Jessica. She was the girl who was all over Brink in Karma a few years back," Meeka's thoughts began to roll, and within seconds she gasped. Paulette nodded her head and laughed.

"I can see it in your eyes you remember her. She was all over Hustle like white on rice." Paulette laughed.

"Yea and I was all over her with that Ciroc bottle. If you wouldn't have grabbed my arm, that bitch would have left out on a stretcher." They both laughed.

"You are still crazy Meeka. I guess some things will never change."

"I'm going to die crazy." Meeka laughed.

***

Meeka slowly walked through her house reminiscing. Every room was full of memories, good and bad. She had to admit it, majority of the memories were good. Today she was moving, and she was happy.

Meeka grabbed her phone and checked the time, and it was 12:30 am. She walked to her mirror and checked her makeup. She powered her nose a little and fluffed her hair. Five minutes later Hustle walked through the door with his MCM book bag in his hand. Meeka could see a tired look scribbled all over his face.

"Hey, baby." She smiled and stood to her feet. Meeka walked over to him and wrapped her arms around his slim neck. He kissed her forehead and grabbed her ass. She didn't have much ass, but he didn't care.

"What's up boo, you like nice." He said.

"Yea and all of it is for you. How did things go?" Meeka asked and pull Hustle to the bed. She pulled his Jordan 11's off and removed his fitted cap from off his head. Then she climbed onto the bed on her knees and pulled his shirt off his body. She began to rub his shoulders and waited for him to give her a few answers.

"It was straight, but I lost about $1,500 at the casino." He chuckled and shook his head.

"Hmmm, that's it?" She laughed.

"Yea, but I won $600 of it back."

"Wow, that is a first." She laughed again.

"It really is. What time are you going to the club to collect?" Hustle asked as he unzipped his pants and wiggled his pants off. He removed Meeka's hands from his

shoulders and stood to his feet. He dropped his boxers to his feet and kicked them to the side. He stood in front of Meeka butt naked, and she enjoyed looking at every inch of his naked body.

"About 2:00 a.m. but if you want me to stay I will." Meeka slipped out of her robe and slowly fell backward on her back. She rubbed her hands against her sexy body and pulled Hustle closer to her with her legs. She loved the sexy look that was in his sexy eyes.

"Go and get that money baby. You know daddy will be here waiting on you." Hustle rubbed his hand against Meeka thighs and climbed on top of her.

"I know daddy, and that's why I love you. Once again I'm sorry, and I never want to make you upset like that again. I hate when you're mad at me." She grabbed his face and kissed his lips.

"Tameeka you know I didn't want to do that shitty ass shit. I never want to share you again. Not even with another bitch."

"I know baby, and I'm sorry for the millionth time you know that I love you. You're my big strong man." She giggled and rubbed his back. Meeka wrapped her legs around Hustle's back and kissed him passionately. She covered his face and chest with soft, but wet kisses. He couldn't handle the affection he was receiving, and he exhaled and rolled over. Meeka flipped her hair and climbed on top of him. As she caressed his body and she could feel his penis becoming hard.

"Why do you love me so much?" Meeka asked. She was breathing heavily, and her hormones were going crazy.

Hustle licked his index and middle finger. Then he entered them into Meeka's vagina. He slowly entered and pulled them out. Meeka rolled her neck and closed her eyes. The way Hustle played with her vagina felt amazing.

"Because you're Tameeka and you're the most amazing woman in the world."

"Oh really!?" Meeka asked sarcastically and giggled. She knew exactly what she was doing. Hustle repeatedly slapped on Meeka's ass while she rubbed her hand against his penis and began to stroke it. He swarmed in the bed, and his toes curled.

"Do that thang I like," Hustle stroked Meeka's hair and moved her head to his dick. She began to pleasure him with oral sex. His big dick and hairy balls were covered with her saliva. Hustle was a sucker for head from Meeka and always became aggressive while she was pleasuring him. He grabbed the back of her head and rammed his dick deeper into her mouth. She gagged loudly, but she continued to pleasure him.

"Damn Meek that feels good." He moaned.

"How good does it feel?" She whispered.

"Good enough to make me forgive you." He chuckled and wiped his face.

"That's what I like to hear." Meeka sucked and slobbered on his dick non-stop. She pretended his dick was a salt grinder and twisted it. She looked over her shoulder and saw that his toes were curling. Meeka was driving Hustle crazy, and he couldn't take much more of her head game. He grabbed her by the neck and pulled her closer to him. He shoved his tongue into her mouth and grabbed his dick. Her pink lipstick was smudged all over their faces. As he kissed her, he gave himself a head job, and his teeth began to chatter.

Meeka started to play with her own pussy and rubbed her breast. Hustle stared at her, he was so turned on.

"Choke me." She licked her lips and moaned to him. He didn't reply, but he softly dug his nails into her neck and did what she asked. Then he sucked on her breast and kissed on her chest. Meeka couldn't control herself anymore. She was ready to feel Hustle inside of her. She grabbed his dick and rammed it into her pussy. She twirled her pussy on his dick and whipped her hair. Meeka bounced on his dick and gripped his shoulders while she made her ass bounce up and down. Hustle slapped her on her ass, leaving his handprints on both cheeks.

"Oh no, you're not going to drive me crazy." Hustle grabbed Meeka and tossed her on the bed. He snatched her hair and positioned her body in the doggy style position.

"Arch your back like you used to do when you were seventeen years old. I want that ass all the way in the air!" Meeka did exactly what Hustle said. Without turning around, she knew he was smiling and enjoying the view.

"Damn, the golden arch, what a wonderful view." He chuckled. Hustle gripped Meeka's hips and shoved his dick deeper and deeper into her pussy. She didn't want to shout, so she buried her face into the sheets and moaned.

"Aaahhhhhh, damn baby that feels so good. Fuck me harder....harder....harder!!" Meeka said.

"Like that baby?" Hustle smiled at the site of Meeka's ass crack. Sweat dripped down his face, and he used his shoulder to wipe his face. He could feel that he was about to explode all inside of her. The closer he got to his climax as he gripped her hips tighter and pulled her hair. He pretended he was a jockey and Meeka was his horse.

"Hmmmmmmmmm, mmmmmmmm, mmmmmmm," he bit his bottom lip and collapsed on top of Meeka. She turned around and asked, *"You're tapping out already?"*

"Yea man, I can't rooster like I use to." They laughed, and he shook his head.

"Your old ass better be ready for round two when I get back." Meeka reached on her nightstand and grabbed a hair tie. She quickly tied her hair into a bun and kissed Hustle on the forehead.

"Old, we're only a few years apart. If I'm old what are you?" He laughed.

Uhhhh, younger than you are duh!" She chuckled, and Hustle laughed and wiped the sweat off of her back.

"Yea, whatever you say Tameeka."

"Bae, I have to tell you something and don't be mad at me." Meeka exhaled and maneuvered to her back.

"Tameeka what did you do?" Hustle sighed and rubbed his head. He tried to get out of bed, but Meeka stopped him.

"Where are you going Brink?" Meeka asked.

"To clean up whatever mess you made. Where the hell are my keys?" Hustle searched the floor for his keys, but he couldn't find them. Meeka pulled on his arm and climbed on top of him.

"Baby I swear, I didn't do anything. I need to tell you something before I tell everyone else."

"Tell me what?" Hustle asked.

"Someone told me Austin is plotting against me."

"What?" Hustle laughed, but Meeka gave him an ugly glare. He noticed Meeka didn't laugh or crack a smile, so he awkwardly cleared his throat and nodded his head at her.

"Anyways, Marlo told me that Forty told him, that he heard that Austin is trying to seek revenge on me. He wants to bring my entire operation down, but I'm not having it. I started this shit when I was twelve years old, and I'm thirty-two years old now. They could never tie me to anything they are trying to accuse me of. I've always had a solid team, and I'll be damn if it crumbles now!"

"Yea and you say that shit like it's a good thing," Hustle said.

"Come on baby, every time you say that I know EXACTLY where this conversation is going." Meeka rolled her eyes and banged her fist into the soft bed. Hustle shook his head and climbed out of bed. He walked to his dresser and grabbed a pair of clean boxers then he walked into the bathroom. Meeka chased after Hustle and entered the bathroom. He ignored her and stepped into the shower. Meeka hesitated, but she entered the shower with him. As he soaked his body with warm water and Dove body wash,

Meeka stood quietly behind him. She knew she had to choose her words carefully. If she didn't, her simple words would lead to his same speech.

"Can we finish talking about what Marlo and Forty said?" Meeka spoke in a low tone. Hustle shook his and turned around. Meeka could taste his attitude, it was so thick. "Brink, I asked you a question, and I would like for you to answer it."

"Talk Tameeka damn, what did Marlo tell Forty and how did he find that out?" Hustle asked.

"I don't know how Marlo and Forty knew any of this. The important thing is that they know and they told me. I tried talking to Justice about it, but she doesn't believe it. She thinks it's just a rumor and her brother wouldn't do that."

"Forget what she thinks. What do you think?"

"I think, scratch that, I know it's true. You remember how angry I told you he was that day. He honestly thinks I'm the reason for their divorce."

"You aren't the reason, and the only reason why I didn't kick his ass is because I know he's dirty! That nigga would have had my ass in jail doing ten years for a crime that I didn't commit." He laughed.

"Exactly, he's DIRTY! He's dirty enough to do anything. You and I have witnessed him ruin people's life within seconds." Meeka banged her open hand against the wet wall. Hustle rubbed her back and squeezed the soapy towel on it. She held onto the wall and rolled her neck she was enjoying how the hot water felt dripping down her body.

"Yea, you are right. This is the last thing we need right now. We just got the plug from Arkansas on our team. We won't need anything fooling with our money flow."

"Hmmm, who are you telling, I have to figure this shit out as soon as possible. Poor Justice, she's so damn stupid and blind. Sometimes her stupidity makes my stomach turn. It can literally make my skin crawl."

"What are you going to do?" Hustle asked.

"I don't know, but first I'm going to get out of this shower before I give you the best blow job ever." Meeka kissed Hustle's neck and got out of the shower. He gently grabbed her hand and said, "Why are you leaving, nothing is wrong with that." He smiled.

"I have to go, but you better get your rest for round two, three, and four. You're going to need it old man." She laughed and covered her body with a towel.

"I'm only five years older than you."

"That's five years closer to God than me." She giggled.

"Seriously though baby, how do you feel about all of this? You really haven't said much." Hustle turned the shower off and waited for Meeka to answer his question. She tossed him the bath towel and stared down at the floor. She really didn't know how to answer his question.

"I – I – I- I don't know. At first, I didn't want to believe it, but I would be a fool if I didn't. I don't understand why he's so angry with me. I'm not the one divorcing him. Like really Brink, is it really that serious?" Meeka sighed and sat on the toilet. She watched as Hustle *patted his naked body with the towel. His balls were jiggling, and his dick was swinging from left to right. Meeka was ready to fuck again, but she quickly shook the thought out of her head and walked out of the bathroom. Before she could step into the room Hustle grabbed her arm and said, "Don't worry yourself about it. Maybe it is just a rumor."*

"But maybe it isn't, then what? What am I going to do?"

"Stop saying you, it's what are WE going to do."

"So what are we going to do?" Meeka asked. She stared at Hustle with an innocent look on her face, and it worried him. It was a look that he has never seen in her eyes before.

"What is wrong is there something else you're not telling me?" Hustle asked.

"No, I'm just really worried. This has never happened to me before, NOT even once. I'm scared of the things Sydney has told him over the years. What if everything goes left? I can't let anything happen to Izzy, I swear Brink I will lose my fucking mind."

"No, no, no, I refuse to let you think like that. Nothing will happen to Izzy, and that's my word."

"Do you promise B? Don't make a promise you can't keep," she said.

"I promise Tameeka. Now stop worrying yourself and go get dressed. I'll be here waiting for you." Hustle slapped Meeka on the ass and smiled. The more she stared into his eyes her smile grew bigger and bigger. She tried to

hide it, but she couldn't control it. Hustle made her feel warm and soft inside. Meeka was so mentally and emotionally damaged from her past that she often built an emotional wall up towards Hustle. Sometimes she hated it, but sometimes she didn't. The life she lived she needed to be cautious and guarded. She often thought about her past so that she would appreciate her presence.

She entered Isabella's room smiling. The room was empty, but there was one toy on the floor. The room smelled of baby lotion and hair care supplies. Meeka leaned against the door frame and exhaled. She could picture Izzy running around her room while Hustle chased after her. Meeka wanted to race to California and give Isabella the biggest hug possible.

A single tear dropped from her eyes, but she wiped it away. She had no reason to be sad anymore.

Five minutes later, Marlo walked into the house. He dapped Meeka and grabbed one of the empty boxes.

"What's up sis, do you need help with anything?" He asked.

"What up Marlo and yea. I have a few things I need to pack downstairs. I think it's the towels in the downstairs bathroom."

"Okay cool," Marlo took a step, but he stopped. He stared at the high ceilings and laughed. The memories were also hitting him as well.

"Man, I'm going to miss this house. The shit we've done in here, I'm taking it to my grave." He laughed.

"Fuckin' right you are, not a single soul can know." Meeka laughed.

"I remember when you first brought this place. You wouldn't take a dime from me, and you wanted to pay for everything yourself."

"That's because I'm the big sister and that's what I was supposed to do. Putting a roof over our head and keeping it was my only concern. People never understood that blood couldn't make us closer. You were always my blood brother and nothing less. When it comes to family, you're the only family I have. This may sound crazy, but I'm okay with that." Meeka said.

"I know, and I love you, sis, believe that. Always believe that whenever you need me I'm coming. I don't care what the situation is."

"I love you more, Marlo. Thank you for always being here for me. I know I put you in a lot of crazy situations and I'm sorry. That was never my intention to dangle with your freedom or safety."

"I am danger, and I never keep my gun on safety. You didn't force me to do anything. I did it because I wanted to. You protect me, and I protect you. That's how the game goes."

"Trust me, I know you're danger." She laughed. "Once I get on that plane, it will be no more 'Money Making Meeka.' Just regular Tameeka with the thirty-inch weave. I can't wait to wrap my arms around my sweet baby girl. God, I miss her so much, you don't understand Marlo."

"I know you do, but that's going to be over shortly. I'm going to be take boxes in the car for you."

"Okay," Meeka said. Marlo grabbed Meeka's keys and shoved a box under his arm.

Meeka did one last walk through of the house and walked to the door. She couldn't believe she was leaving behind her old life and starting a new one. On the same note, she was proud of herself for the leap of faith she was taking. She was finally giving Hustle what he wanted, and that's all that mattered.

"Mrs. Money Making Meeka has left the building."

Made in the USA
Monee, IL
22 April 2022